THE CASAGRANDES

"ANYTHING FOR FAMILIA"

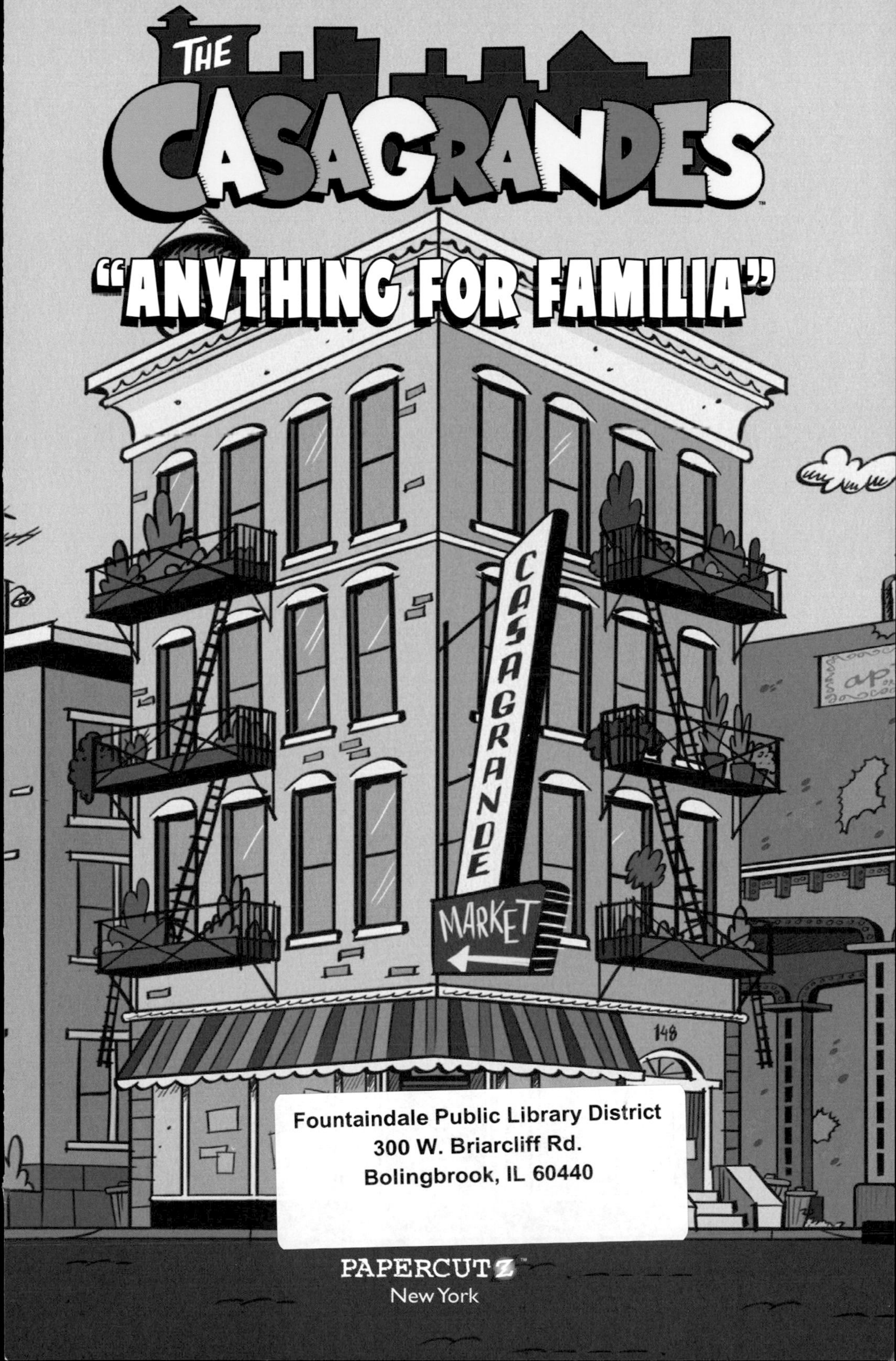
CASAGRANDE
MARKET
148

PAPERCUTZ
New York

THE CASAGRANDES

#2 "ANYTHING FOR FAMILIA"

nickelodeon THE CASAGRANDES #2 “ANYTHING FOR FAMILIA

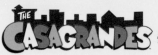

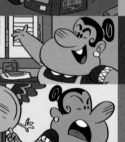

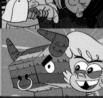

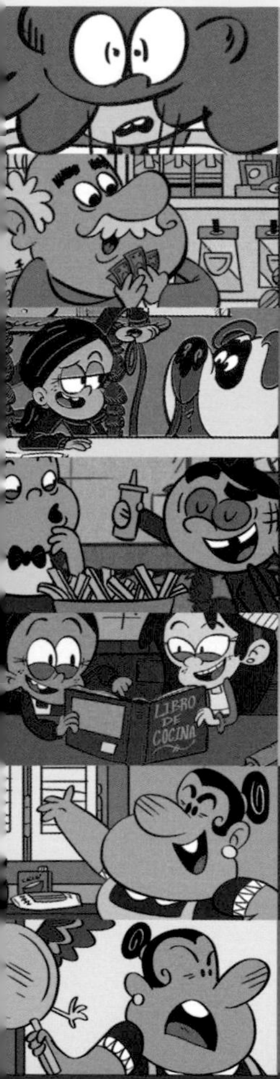

“CITY TRICKERS”
Andrew Brooks — Writer
Gizelle Orbino — Artist, Colorist
Wilson Ramos Jr. — Letterer

“MISSION IMPAWSIBLE”
Amanda Fein — Writer
Jennifer Hernandez— Artist, Colorist
Wilson Ramos Jr. — Letterer

“CUSTOMER APPRECIATION DAY”
Kiernan Sjursen-Lien — Writer
Jose Hernandez — Artist, Colorist
Wilson Ramos Jr. — Letterer

“PARTY ANIMALS”
Derek Fridolfs — Writer
Chris Sabatino — Artist
Zazo Aguiar — Colorist
Wilson Ramos Jr. — Letterer

“LOST AND FOUND”
Diem Doan
Writer, Artist, Colorist, Letterer

“COMIC RELIEF”
Cailtin Fein — Writer
Zazo Aguiar — Artist, Colorist
Wilson Ramos Jr. — Letterer

“LET'S KETCHUP”
[illegible] — Writer
[illegible] — Artist, Colorist
Wilson Ramos Jr. — Letterer

“CASA CAMPERS”
Kristen G. Smith — Writer
Kelsey Wooley— Artist, Colorist
Wilson Ramos Jr. — Letterer

“A GLITTERING RECIPE”
Julia Rothenburger-Garcia — Writer
Tyler Koberstein — Artist, Colorist
Wilson Ramos Jr. — Letterer

“¡TU DESTINO!”
Kristen G. Smith — Writer
Ron Bradley— Artist, Colorist
Wilson Ramos Jr. — Letterer

“COOKING WITH THE CASAGRANDES”
Gabrielle Dolbey
Writer, Artist, Colorist, Letterer

[illegible]

“SNACK ATTACK”
Kiernan Sjursen-Lien — Writer
Daniela Rodriguez — Artist, Colorist
Wilson Ramos Jr. — Letterer

“UNBREAK-A-BULL”
Ron Bradley — Writer, Artist, Colorist
Wilson Ramos Jr. — Letterer

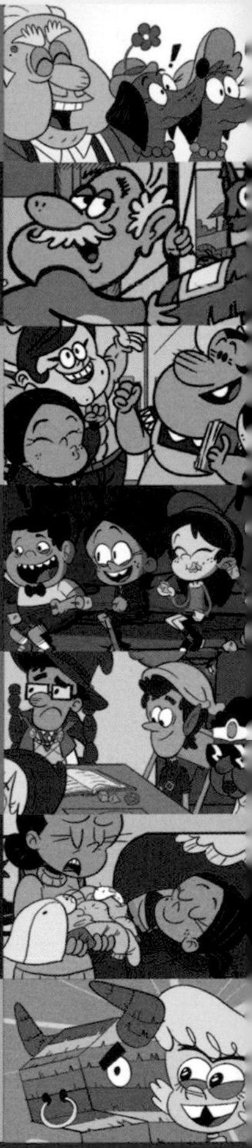

RON BRADLEY — Cover Artist
JAMES SALERNO — Sr. Art Director/Nickelodeon
JAYJAY JACKSON — Design
KRISTEN G. SMITH, DANA CLUVERIUS, MOLLIE FREILICH, NEIL WADE, MIGUEL PUGA, LALO ALCARAZ, KRISTEN YU-UM, EMILIE CRUZ, and MICOL HIATT — Special Thanks
JEFF WHITMAN — Editor
LILY LU — Editorial Intern
JOAN HILTY — Comics Editor/Nickelodeon
ARTHUR “DJ” DESIN — Comics Coordinator/Nickelodeon
JIM SALICRUP
Editor-in-Chief

ISBN: 978-1-5458-0863-4 paperback edition
ISBN: 978-1-5458-0862-7 hardcover edition

www.papercutz.com

Papercutz books may be purchased for business or promotional use. For information on bulk purchases please contact Macmillan Corporate and Premium Sales Department at (800) 221-7945 x5442.

Printed in Turkey by Elma Basim
February 2022

Distributed by Macmillan
First Printing

THE CASAGRANDES

Theme Song Performed by: ALLY BROOKE
Theme Song Composed by: GERMAINE FRANCO
Lyrics by: GERMAINE FRANCO, MIKE RUBINER & LALO ALCARAZ
Rap Lyrics Performed by: IZABELLA ALVAREZ

I'm in the big city with my big familia [family]

Everyday here is my favorite dia [day]

One big house and our family store
Food and laughter ¡y mucho amor! [and a lot of love!]

Tíos [aunts and uncles], abuelos [grandparents], all of my primos [cousins]...

A dog, a parrot, amigos! [friends!]

We're one big family now!
Sundays and Mondays
They're all fun days when you're with the...
Casagrandes!
¡Mucha vida! [A lot of life!]

Casagrandes!
¡Bienvenida! [Welcome!]

Casagrandes!
¡Mucha risa! [A lot of laughs!]

Casagrandes!
We're all familia! [Family!]

¡Tan-tan! [Tah-dah!]

MEET THE CASAGRANDES

and friends!

RONNIE ANNE SANTIAGO

Ronnie Anne's a skateboarding city girl now. She's fearless, free-spirited, and always quick to come up with a plan. She's one tough cookie, but she also has a sweet side. Ronnie Anne loves helping her family, and that's taught her to help others too. When she's not pitching in at the family *mercado*, you can find her exploring the neighborhood with her best friend Sid, or ordering hot dogs with her skater buds Casey, Nikki, and Sameer. Having a family as big as the Casagrandes has taught Ronnie Anne to deal with anything life throws her way.

BOBBY SANTIAGO

Bobby is Ronnie Anne's big bro. He's a student and one of the hardest workers in the city. He loves his family and loves working at the *mercado*. As his *abuelo's* right hand man, Bobby can't wait to take over the family business one day. He's a big kid at heart, and his clumsiness gets him into some sticky situations at work, like locking himself in the freezer. Mercado mishaps aside, everyone in the neighborhood loves to come to the store and talk to Bobby.

MARIA CASAGRANDE SANTIAGO

Maria is Bobby and Ronnie Anne's mom. As a nurse at the city hospital, she's hardworking and even harder to gross out. For years, Maria, Bobby, and Ronnie Anne were used to only having each other… but now that they've moved in with their Casagrande relatives, they're embracing big family life. Maria is the voice of reason in the household and known for her always-on-the-go attitude. Her long work hours means she doesn't always get to spend time with Bobby and Ronnie Anne; but when she does, she makes that time count.

HECTOR CASAGRANDE

Hector is Carlos and Maria's dad, and the *abuelo* of the family (that means grandpa)! He owns the *mercado* on the ground floor of their apartment building and takes great pride in his work, his family, and being the unofficial "mayor" of the block. He loves to tell stories, share his ideas, and gossip (even though he won't admit to it). You can find him working in the *mercado*, playing guitar, or watching his favorite *telenovela*.

ROSA CASAGRANDE

Rosa is Carlos and Maria's mom and the *abuela* of the family (that means grandma)! She's the head of the household, the wisest Casagrande, and the master cook with a superhuman ability to tell when anyone in the house is hungry. She often tries to fix problems or illnesses with traditional Mexican home remedies and potions. She's very protective of her family… sometimes a little too much.

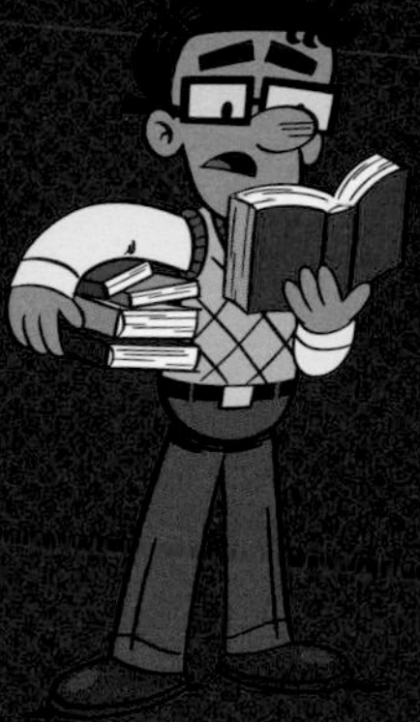

CARLOS CASAGRANDE

Carlos is Maria's brother. He's married to Frida, and together they have four kids: Carlota, C.J., Carl, and Carlitos. Carlos is a Professor of Cultural Studies at a local college. Usually he has his head in the clouds or his nose in a textbook. Relatively easygoing, Carlos is a loving father and an enthusiastic teacher who tries to get his kids interested in their Mexican heritage.

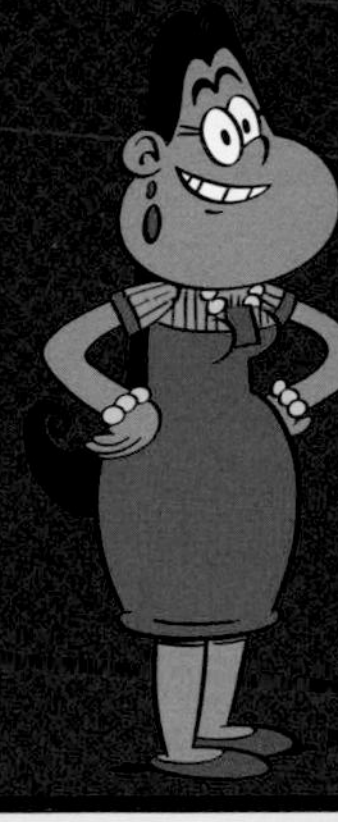

FRIDA PUGA CASAGRANDE

Frida is Carlota, C.J., Carl, and Carlitos' mom. She's an art professor and a performance artist, and is always looking for new ways to express herself. She's got a big heart and isn't shy about her emotions. Frida tends to cry when she's sad, happy, angry, or any other emotion you can think of. She's always up for fun, is passionate about her art, and loves her family more than anything.

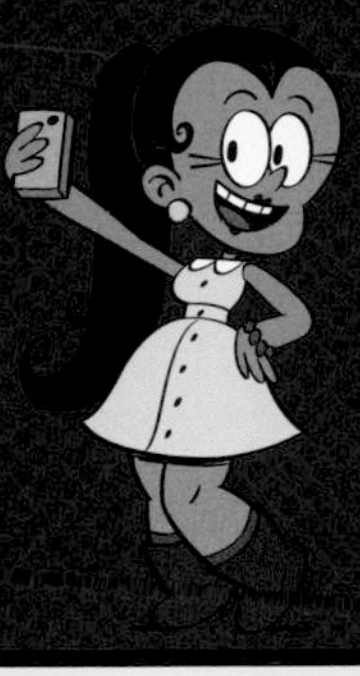

CARLOTA CASAGRANDE

Carlota is CJ, Carl, and Carlitos' older sister. A social media influencer, she's excited to be like a big sister to Ronnie Anne. She's a force to be reckoned with, and is always trying to share her distinctive vintage style tips with Ronnie Anne.

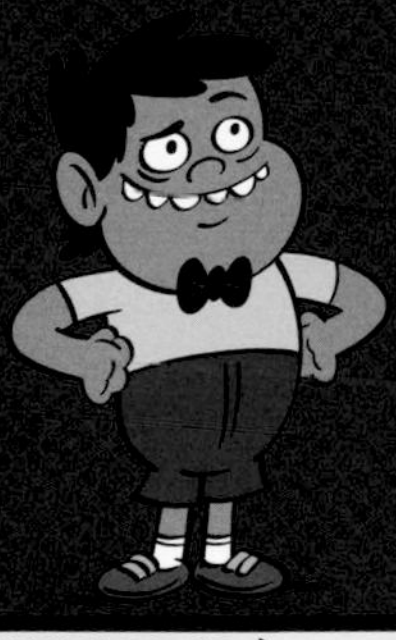

CJ (CARLOS JR.) CASAGRANDE

CJ is Carlota's younger brother and Carl and Carlitos' older brother. He was born with Down Syndrome. He lights up any room with his infectious smile and is always ready to play. He's obsessed with pirates and is BFFs with Bobby. He likes to wear a bowtie to any family occasion, and you can always catch him laughing or helping his *abuela*.

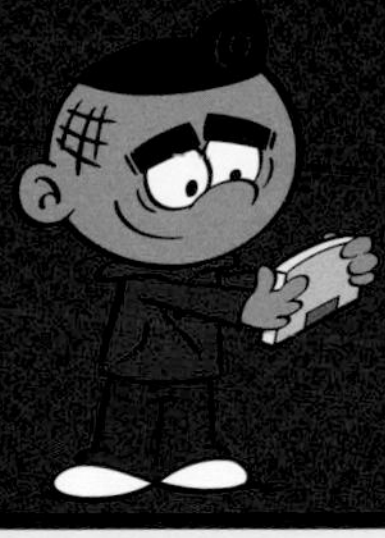

CARL CASAGRANDE

Carl is wise beyond his years. He's confident, outgoing, and puts a lot of time and effort into looking good. He likes to think of himself as a suave businessman and doesn't like to get caught playing with his action figures or wearing his footie PJs. Even though Bobby is nothing but nice to him, Carl sees his big cousin as his biggest rival.

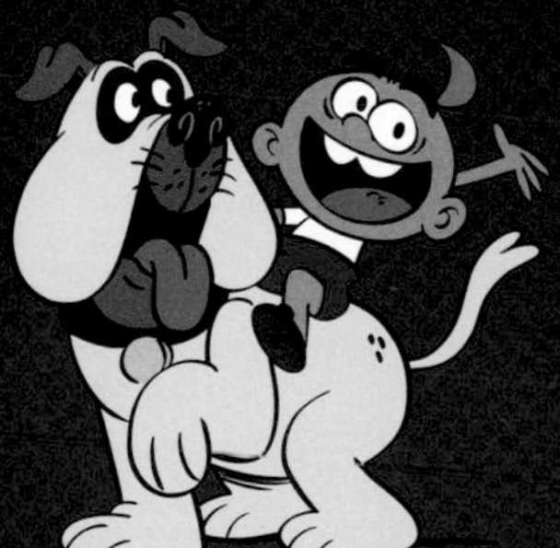

CARLITOS CASAGRANDE

Carlitos is the baby of the family, and is always copying the behavior of everyone in the household—even if they aren't human. He's a playful and silly baby who loves to play with the family pets.

LALO

Lalo is a slobbery bull mastiff who thinks he's a lapdog. He's not the smartest pup, and gets scared easily… but he loves his family and loves to cuddle.

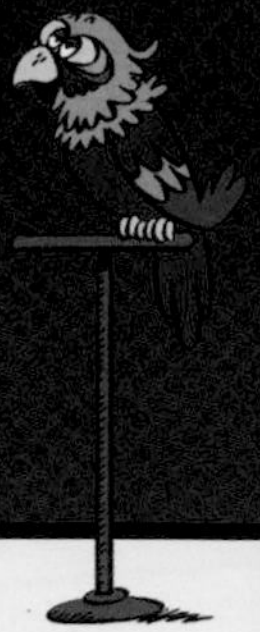

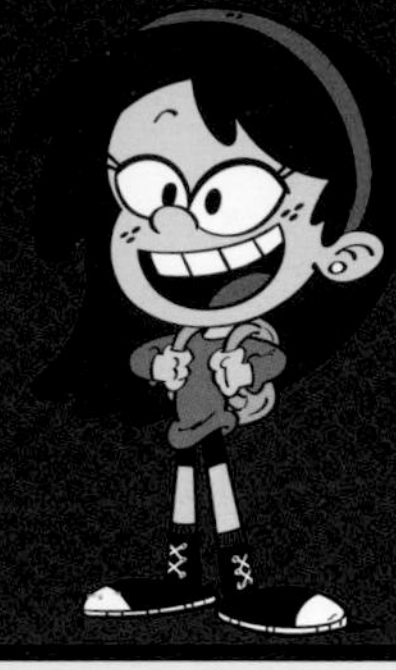

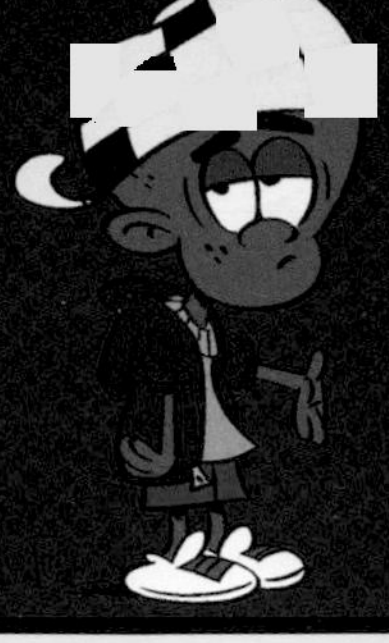

SERGIO

Sergio is the Casagrandes' beloved pet parrot. He's a blunt, sassy bird who "thinks" he's full of wisdom and always has something to say. The Casagrandes have to keep a close eye on their credit card as Sergio is addicted to online shopping and is always asking the family to buy him some new gadget he saw on TV. Sergio is most loyal to Rosa and serves as her wing-man, partner-in-crime, taste-tester, and confidant. Sergio is quite popular in the neighborhood and is always up for a good time. When he's not working part time at the *mercado* (aka messing with Bobby), he can be found hanging with his roommate Ronnie Anne, partying with Sancho and his other pigeon pals, or trying to get his ex-girlfriend, Priscilla (an ostrich at the zoo), to respond to him.

SID CHANG

Sid is Ronnie Anne's quirky best friend. She's new to the city but dives headfirst into everything she finds interesting. She and her family just moved into the apartment one floor above the Casagrandes. In fact, Sid's bedroom is right above Ronnie Anne's. A dream come true for any BFFs.

CASEY

Casey is a happy-go-lucky kid who's always there to help. He knows all the best spots to get grub in Great Lakes City. When he is not skateboarding with the crew, he loves working with his dad, Alberto, on their Cubano sandwich food truck.

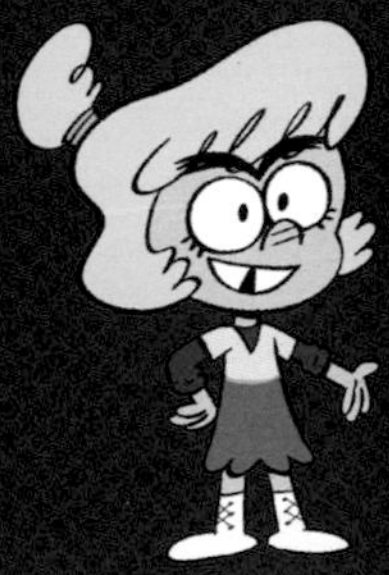

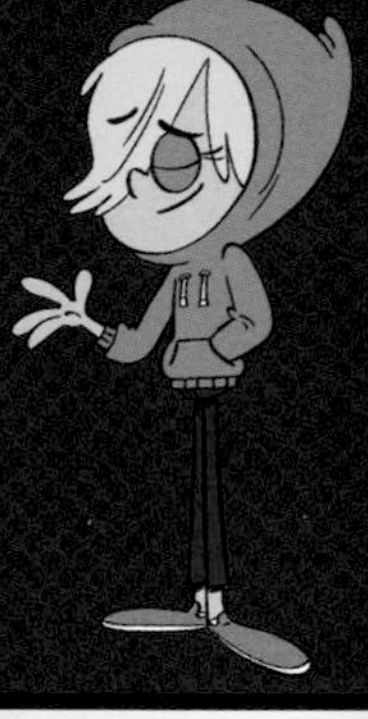

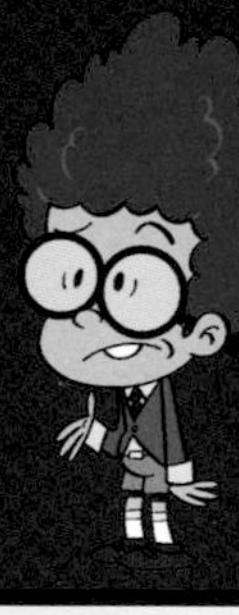

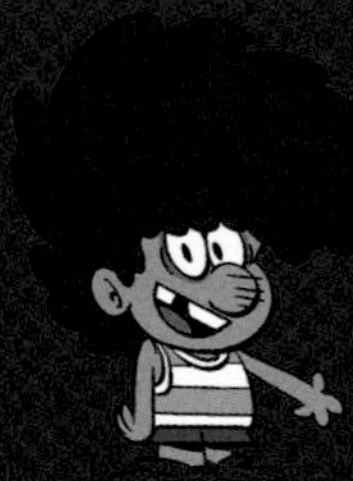

SAMEER

Sameer is a goofy sweetheart who wishes he was taller, but what he lacks in height, he makes up for with his impressive hair and sweet skate moves. He is always down for the unexpected adventure and loves entertaining his friends with his spooky tales!

NIKKI

Nikki is as daring as she is easygoing and laughs when she is nervous. When she's not hanging with her buds at the skatepark, she likes checking out the newest sneakers and reading books about the paranormal.

LAIRD

Laird is a total team player and the newest member of Ronnie Anne's friends. Despite often being on the wrong end of misfortune, Laird is an awesome skateboarder who can do tons of tricks…unfortunately stopping is not one of them.

BECKY

A tough as nails classmate of Ronnie Anne and the skater kids. She makes a good match for her girlfriend, Dodge, captain of the Chavez Academy dodgeball team. Becky has a taste for chaos and destruction that she shares with her younger brother, Ricky, and her loyal dog, Malo. In a pinch though, Becky will definitely come through for a friend in need!

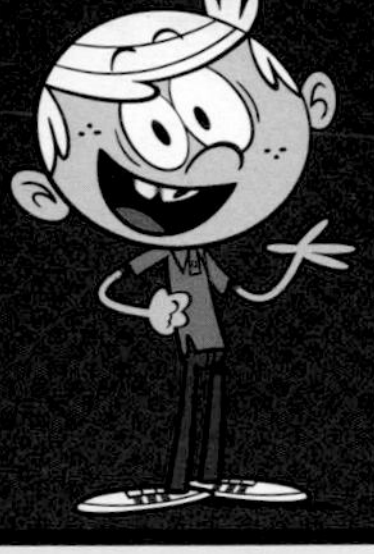

LINCOLN LOUD

Lincoln is Ronnie Anne's dearest friend from Royal Woods. They still keep in touch and visit one another as often as they can. He has learned that surviving the Loud household with ten sisters means staying a step ahead. He's the man with a plan, always coming up with a way to get what he wants or deal with a problem, even if things inevitably go wrong. Lincoln's sisters may drive him crazy, but he loves them and is always willing to help out if they need him.

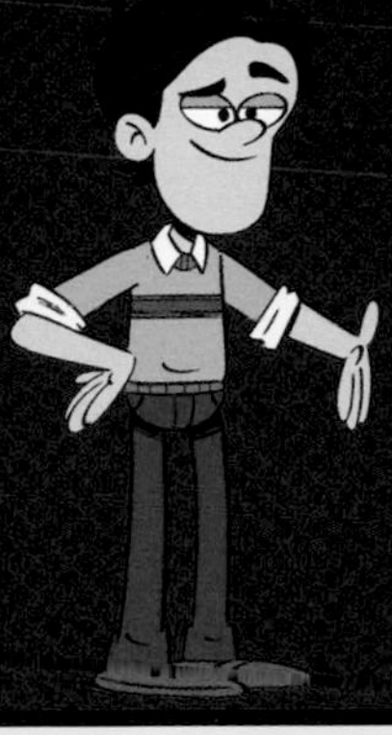

STANLEY CHANG

Stanley Chang is Sid's dad. He's a conductor on the GLART-train that runs through the city. He's a patient man who likes to do Tai Chi when he gets stressed out. He likes to cheer up train commuters with fun facts, but emotionally he breaks down more than the train does.

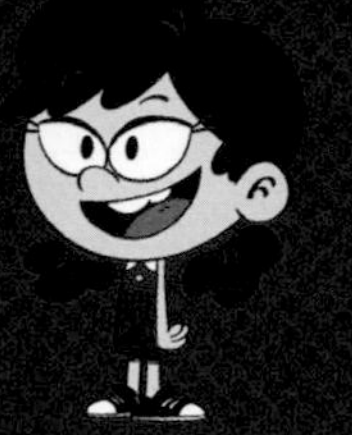

ADELAIDE CHANG

Adelaide Chang is Sid's little sister. She's 6 years old, and has a flair for the dramatic. You can always find her trying to make her way into her big sister Sid's adventures.

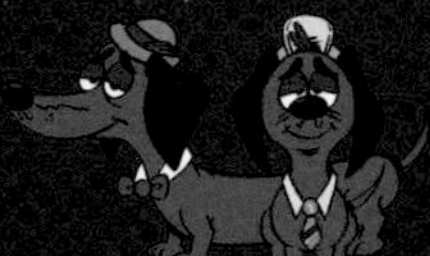

BIG TONY & LITTLE SAL

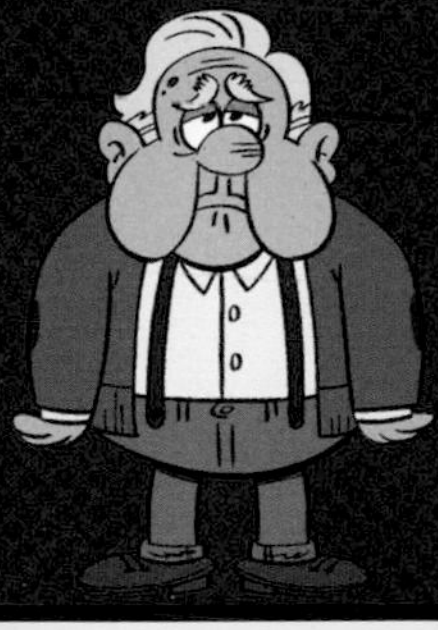

VITO FILLIPONIO

Vito is one of Rosa and Hector's oldest and dearest friends, and a frequent customer at the Mercado. He's lovable, nosy, and usually overstays his welcome, but there is nothing he wouldn't do for his loved ones and his dogs, Big Tony and Little Sal.

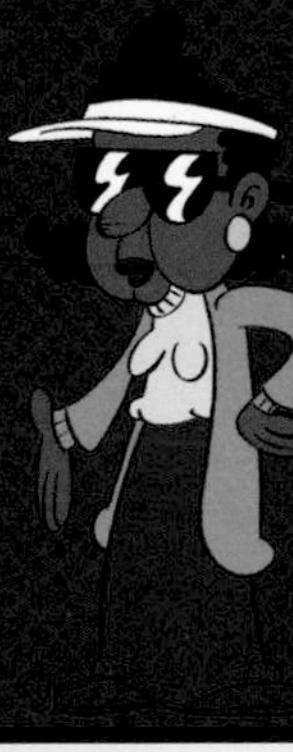

MAYBELLE

Maybelle is a cranky neighborhood regular at the *Mercado* who is obsessed with mangoes. They might be the only thing she eats! Her other loves include movie heartthrob Javier Luna and a good deal. Maybelle is very picky and never misses a chance to complain, but the Casagrandes love her dearly.

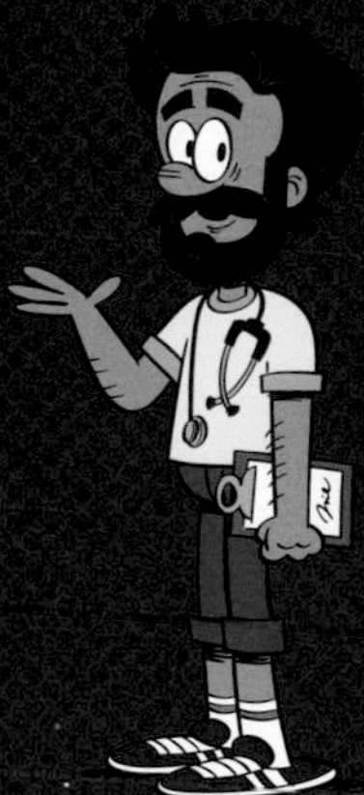

DR. ARTURO SANTIAGO

Arturo is amicably divorced from Ronnie Anne and Bobby's mother Maria, and he is a physician who was previously living and working in Peru with Physicians on Missions, an organization that cares for children and provides vaccines and health care in clinics throughout the world. Like his daughter, Dr. Santiago is adventurous, funny, kindhearted, and charismatic. He and Ronnie Anne share a special bond despite the (previous) distance. And you can definitely see where Bobby gets his silliness from! Even Hector can't help but smile when Arturo joins in on the fun.

"CITY TRICKERS"

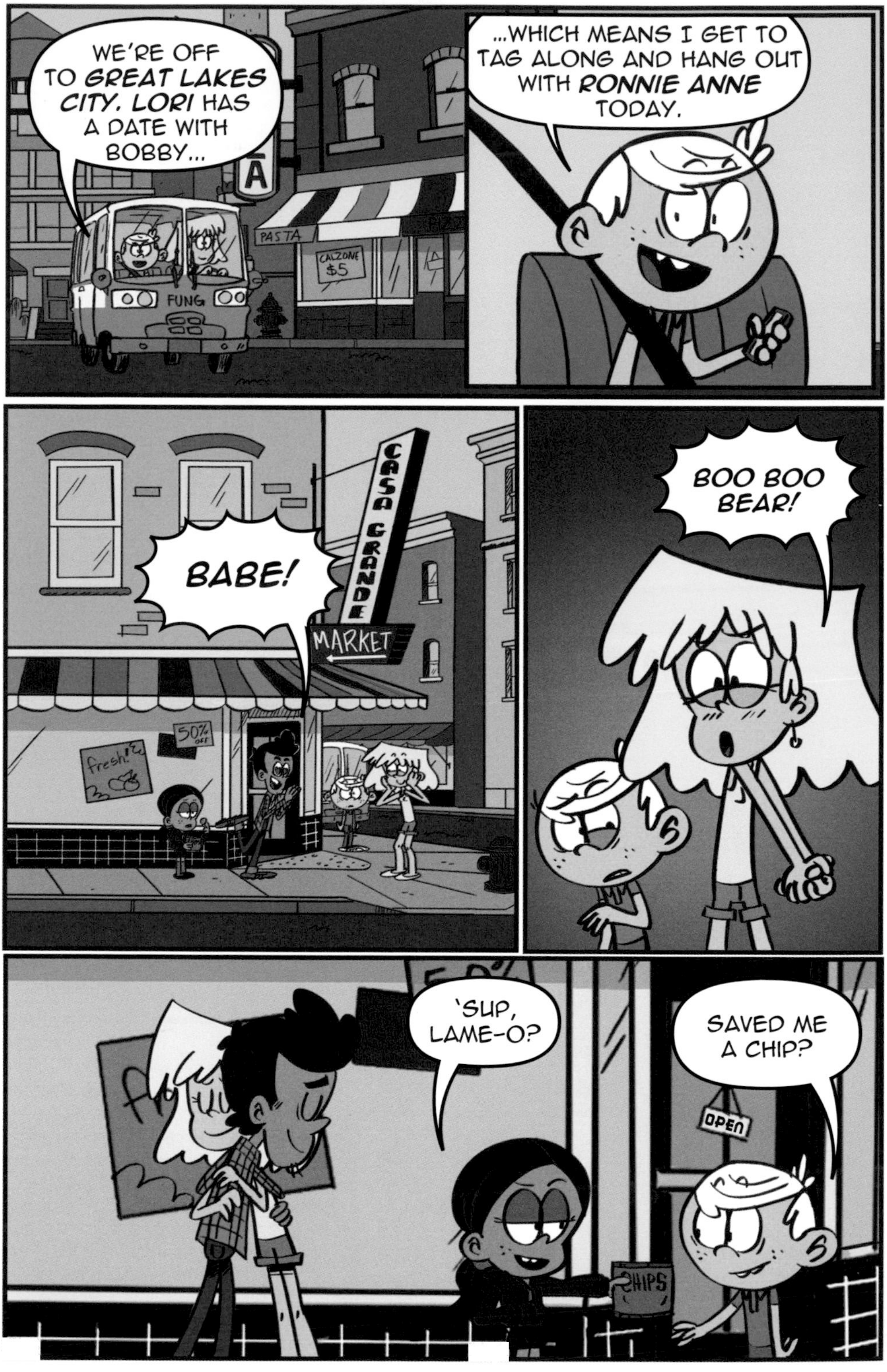
WE'RE OFF TO GREAT LAKES CITY. LORI HAS A DATE WITH BOBBY...
PASTA
CALZONE $5
FUNG
...WHICH MEANS I GET TO TAG ALONG AND HANG OUT WITH RONNIE ANNE TODAY.
CASA GRANDE
MARKET
BABE!
50% OFF
fresh!
BOO BOO BEAR!
'SUP, LAME-O?
SAVED ME A CHIP?
OPEN
CHIPS

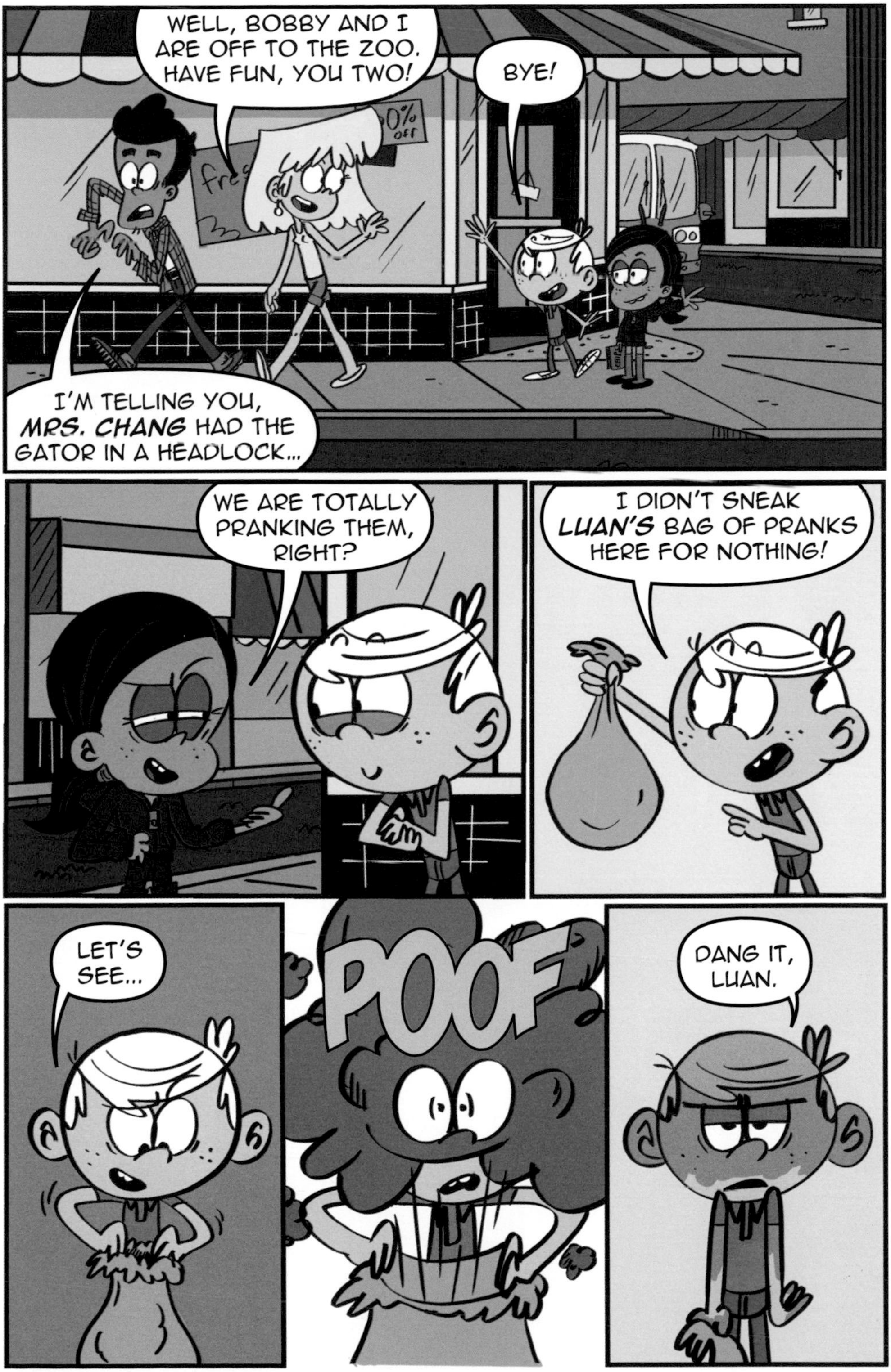
WELL, BOBBY AND I ARE OFF TO THE ZOO. HAVE FUN, YOU TWO!
BYE!
I'M TELLING YOU, MRS. CHANG HAD THE GATOR IN A HEADLOCK...
WE ARE TOTALLY PRANKING THEM, RIGHT?
I DIDN'T SNEAK LUAN'S BAG OF PRANKS HERE FOR NOTHING!
LET'S SEE...
POOF
DANG IT, LUAN.

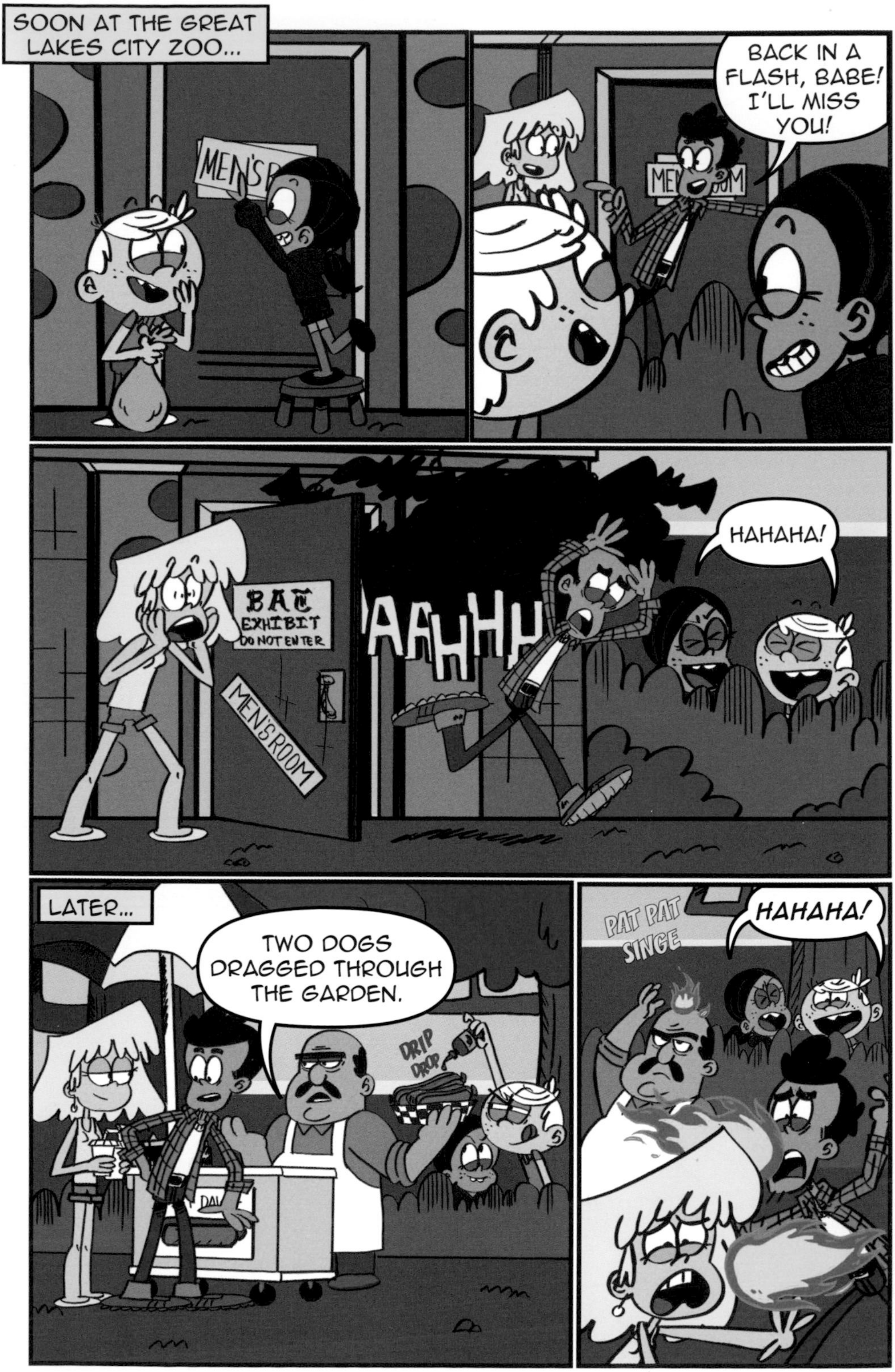

SOON AT THE GREAT LAKES CITY ZOO...
MEN'S R
BACK IN A FLASH, BABE! I'LL MISS YOU!
BAT EXHIBIT DO NOT ENTER
MEN'S ROOM
AAHHH
HAHAHA!
LATER...
TWO DOGS DRAGGED THROUGH THE GARDEN.
DRIP DROP
PAT PAT SINGE
HAHAHA!

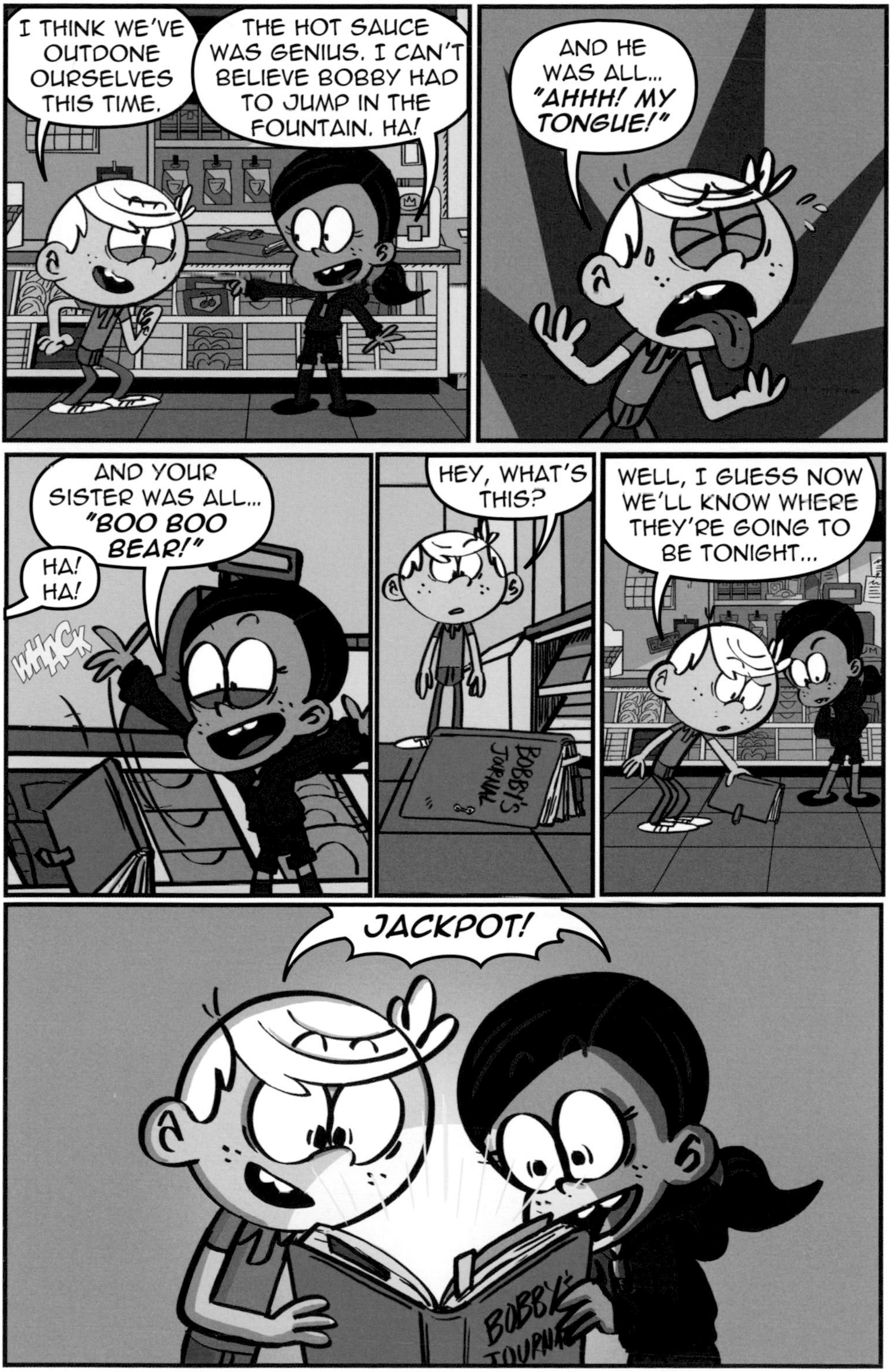
I THINK WE'VE OUTDONE OURSELVES THIS TIME.
THE HOT SAUCE WAS GENIUS. I CAN'T BELIEVE BOBBY HAD TO JUMP IN THE FOUNTAIN. HA!
AND HE WAS ALL... "AHHH! MY TONGUE!"
AND YOUR SISTER WAS ALL... "BOO BOO BEAR!"
HA! HA!
WHACK
HEY, WHAT'S THIS?
BOBBY'S JOURNAL
WELL, I GUESS NOW WE'LL KNOW WHERE THEY'RE GOING TO BE TONIGHT...
JACKPOT!

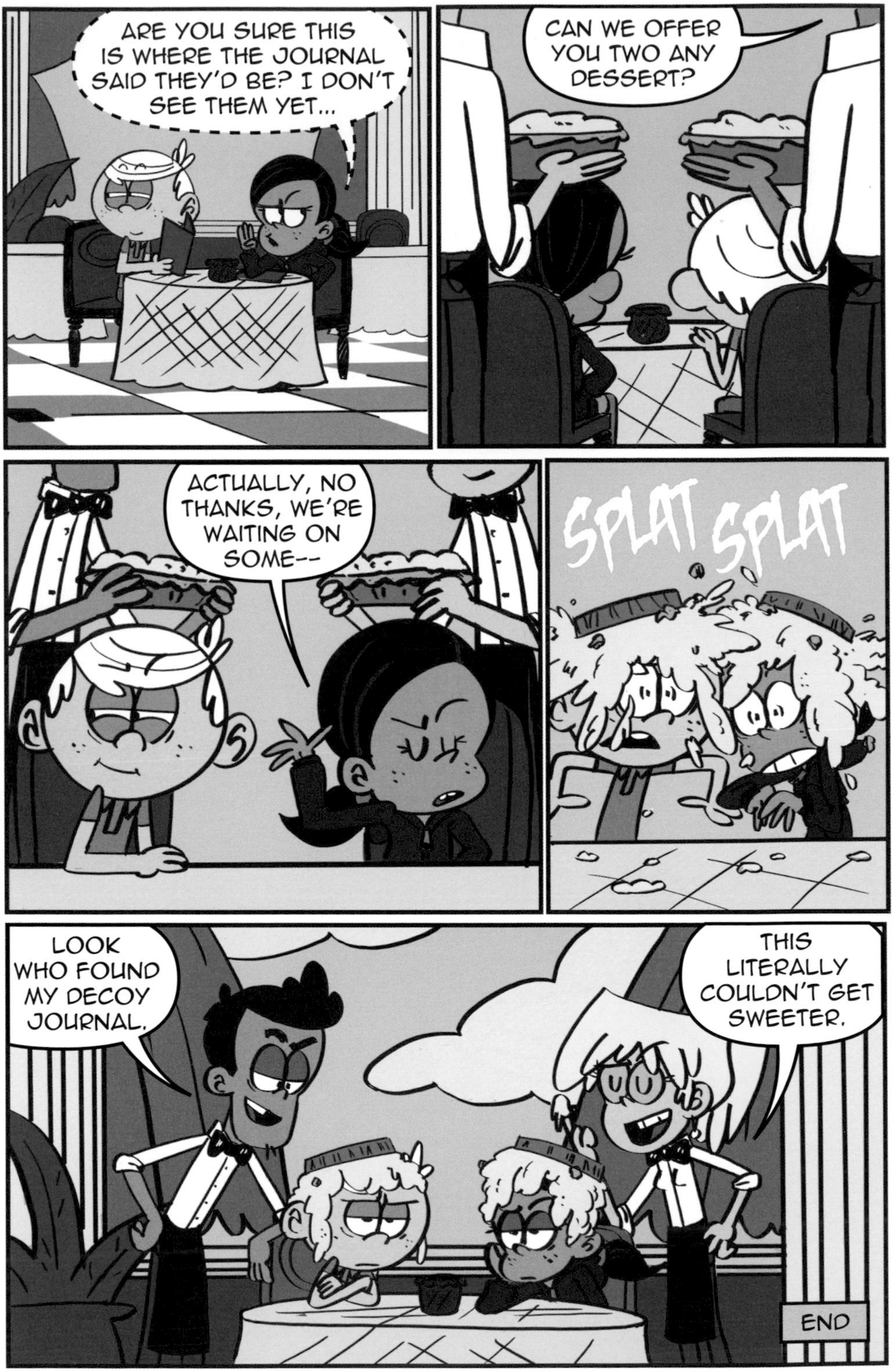
ARE YOU SURE THIS IS WHERE THE JOURNAL SAID THEY'D BE? I DON'T SEE THEM YET...
CAN WE OFFER YOU TWO ANY DESSERT?
ACTUALLY, NO THANKS, WE'RE WAITING ON SOME--
SPLAT SPLAT
LOOK WHO FOUND MY DECOY JOURNAL.
THIS LITERALLY COULDN'T GET SWEETER.
END

"CUSTOMER APPRECIATION"

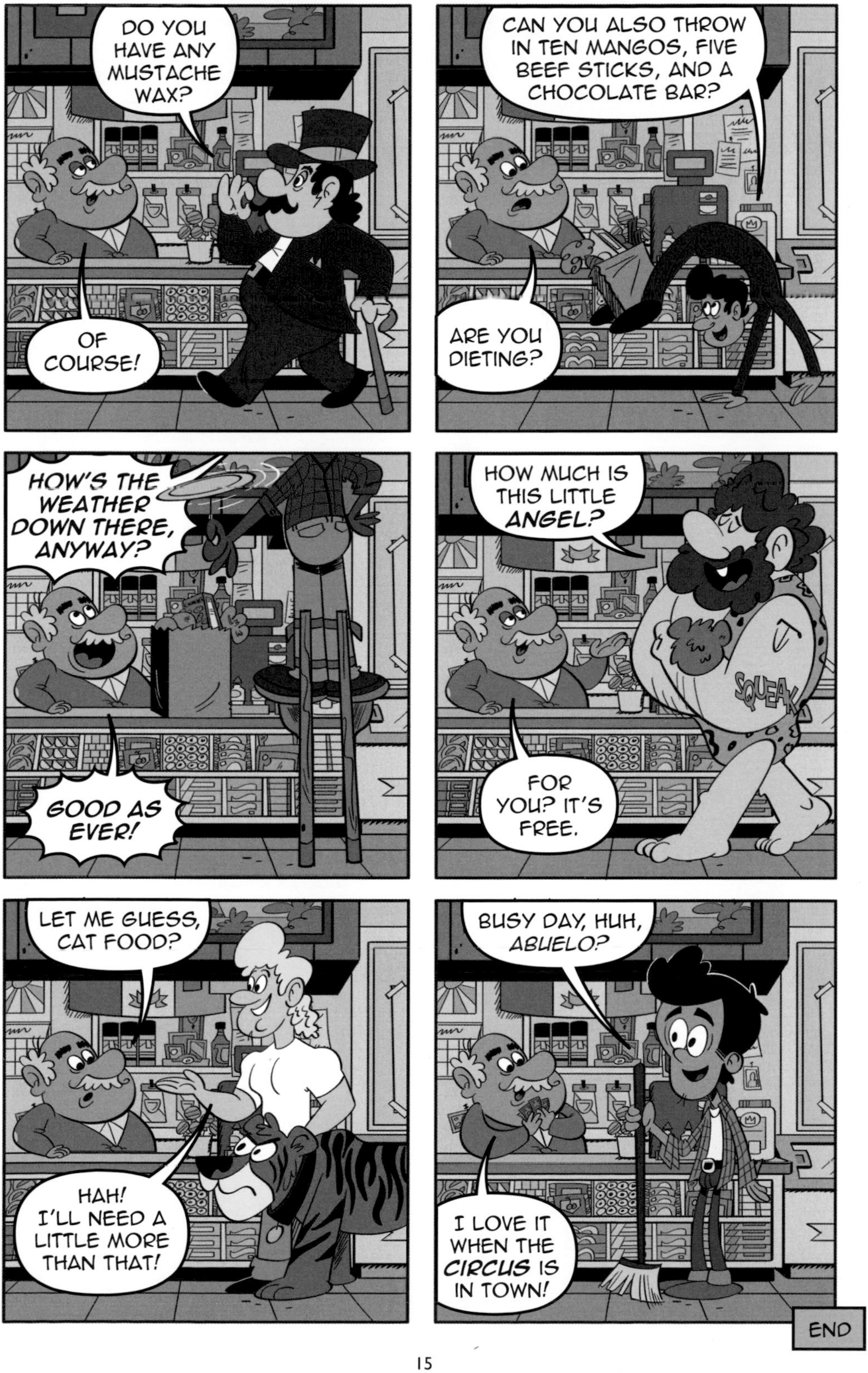
DO YOU HAVE ANY MUSTACHE WAX?
OF COURSE!
CAN YOU ALSO THROW IN TEN MANGOS, FIVE BEEF STICKS, AND A CHOCOLATE BAR?
ARE YOU DIETING?
HOW'S THE WEATHER DOWN THERE, ANYWAY?
GOOD AS EVER!
HOW MUCH IS THIS LITTLE ANGEL?
SQUEAK
FOR YOU? IT'S FREE.
LET ME GUESS, CAT FOOD?
HAH! I'LL NEED A LITTLE MORE THAN THAT!
BUSY DAY, HUH, ABUELO?
I LOVE IT WHEN THE CIRCUS IS IN TOWN!

END

"LOST AND FOUND"

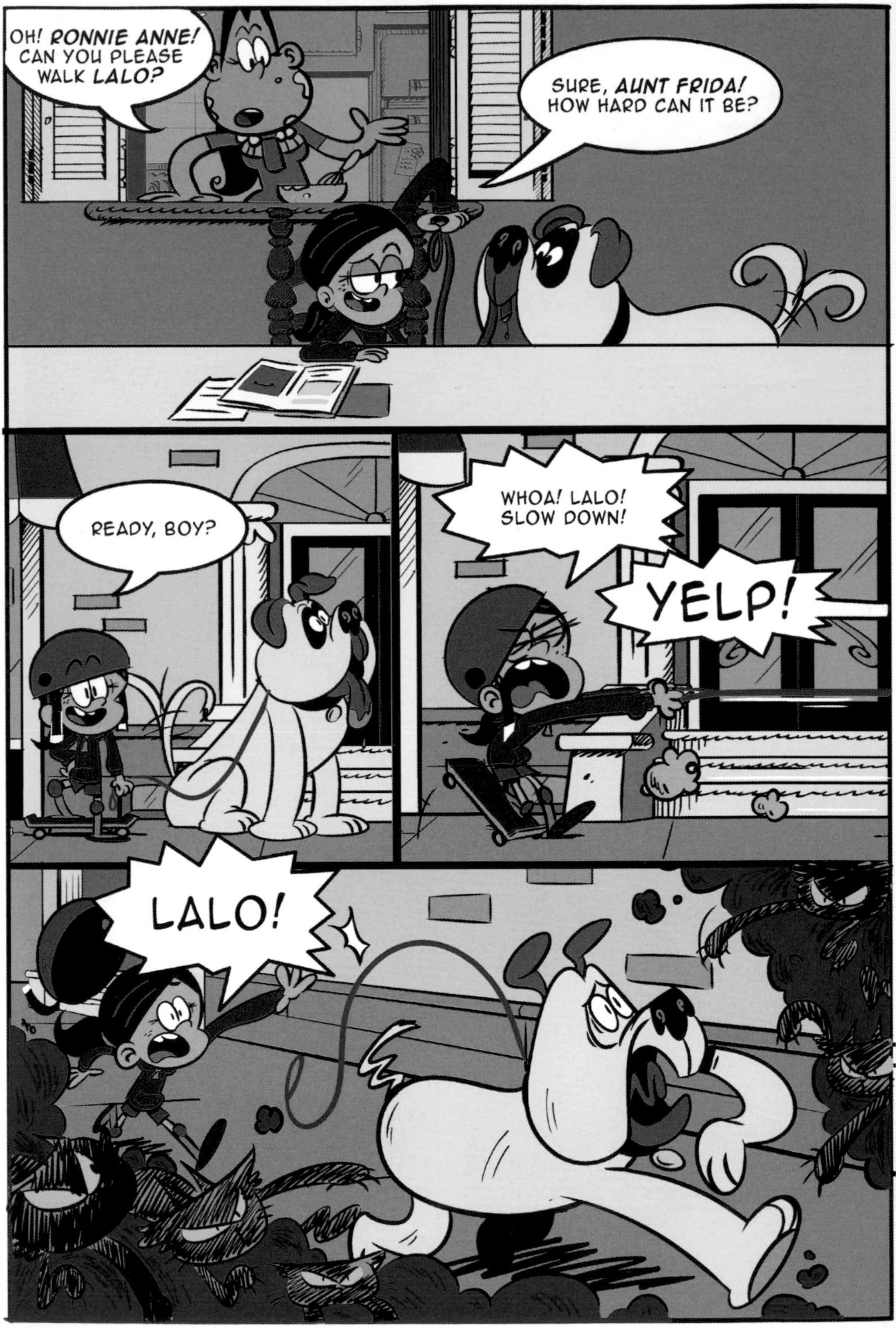
OH! RONNIE ANNE! CAN YOU PLEASE WALK LALO?
SURE, AUNT FRIDA! HOW HARD CAN IT BE?
READY, BOY?
WHOA! LALO! SLOW DOWN!
YELP!
LALO!

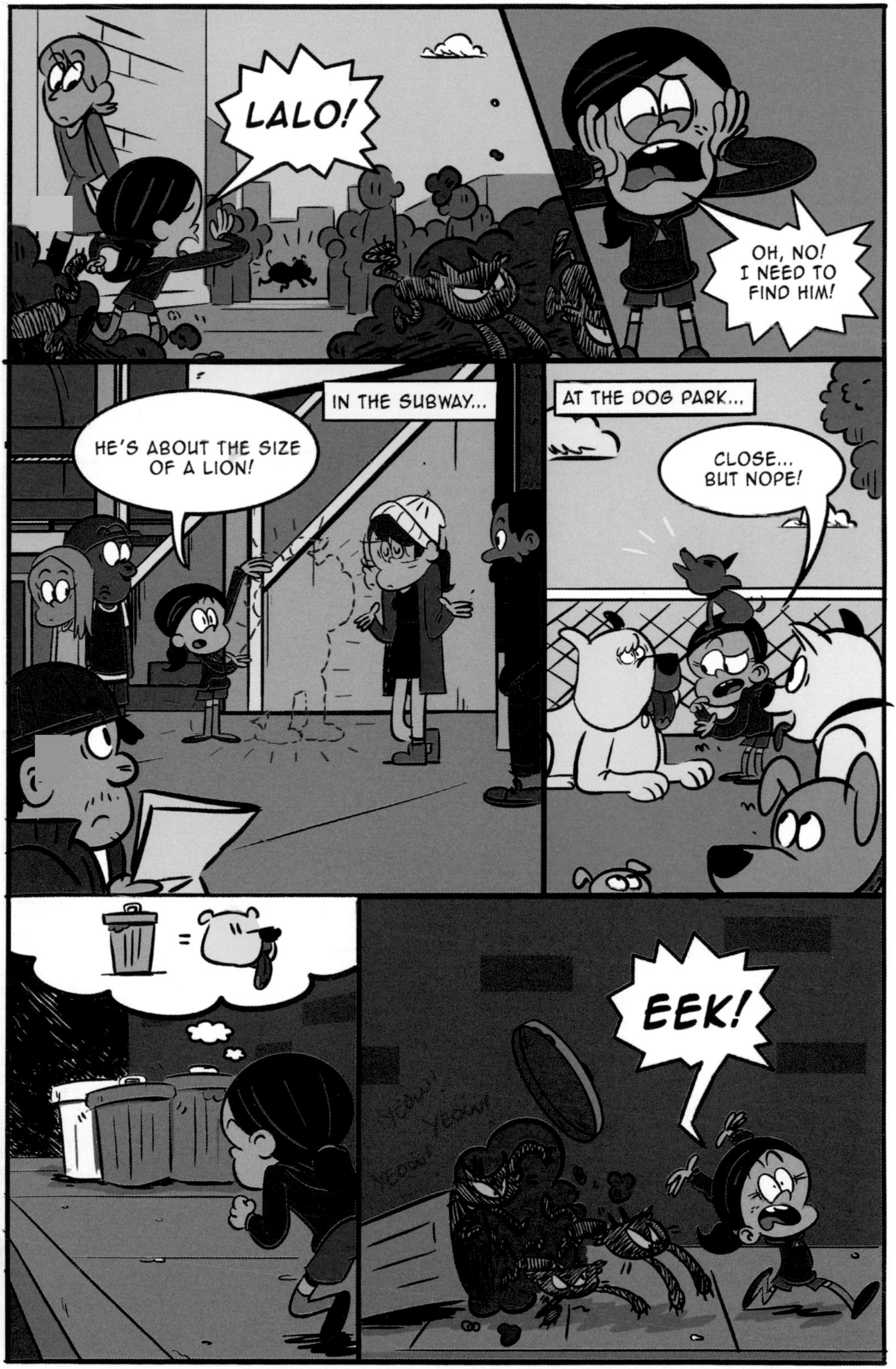
LALO!
OH, NO! I NEED TO FIND HIM!
IN THE SUBWAY...
HE'S ABOUT THE SIZE OF A LION!
AT THE DOG PARK...
CLOSE... BUT NOPE!
EEK!

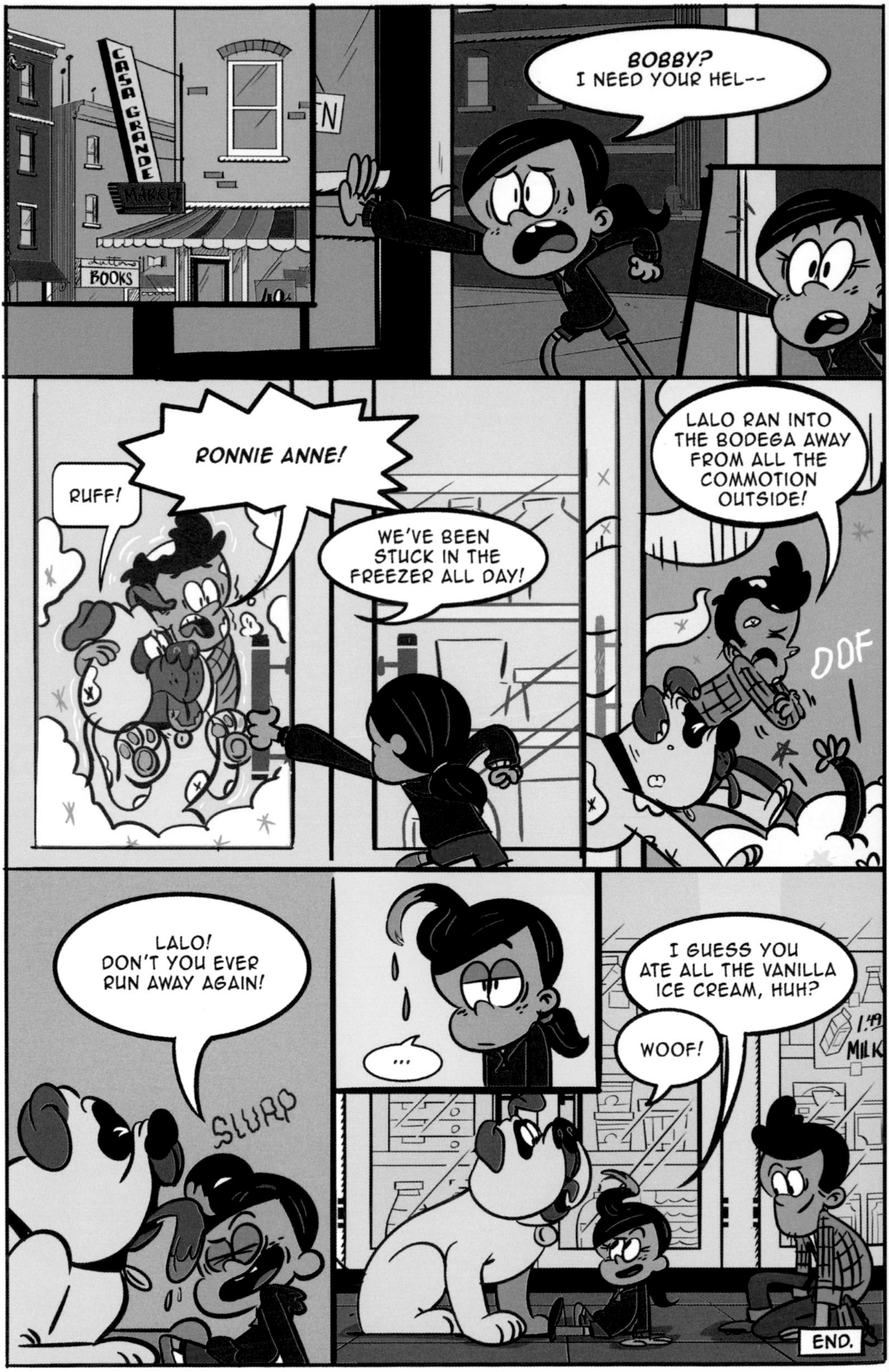
CASA GRANDE
MARKET
BOOKS
BOBBY? I NEED YOUR HEL--
RONNIE ANNE!
RUFF!
WE'VE BEEN STUCK IN THE FREEZER ALL DAY!
LALO RAN INTO THE BODEGA AWAY FROM ALL THE COMMOTION OUTSIDE!
OOF
LALO! DON'T YOU EVER RUN AWAY AGAIN!
SLURP
...
I GUESS YOU ATE ALL THE VANILLA ICE CREAM, HUH?
WOOF!
1.49
MILK
END.

"LET'S KETCHUP"

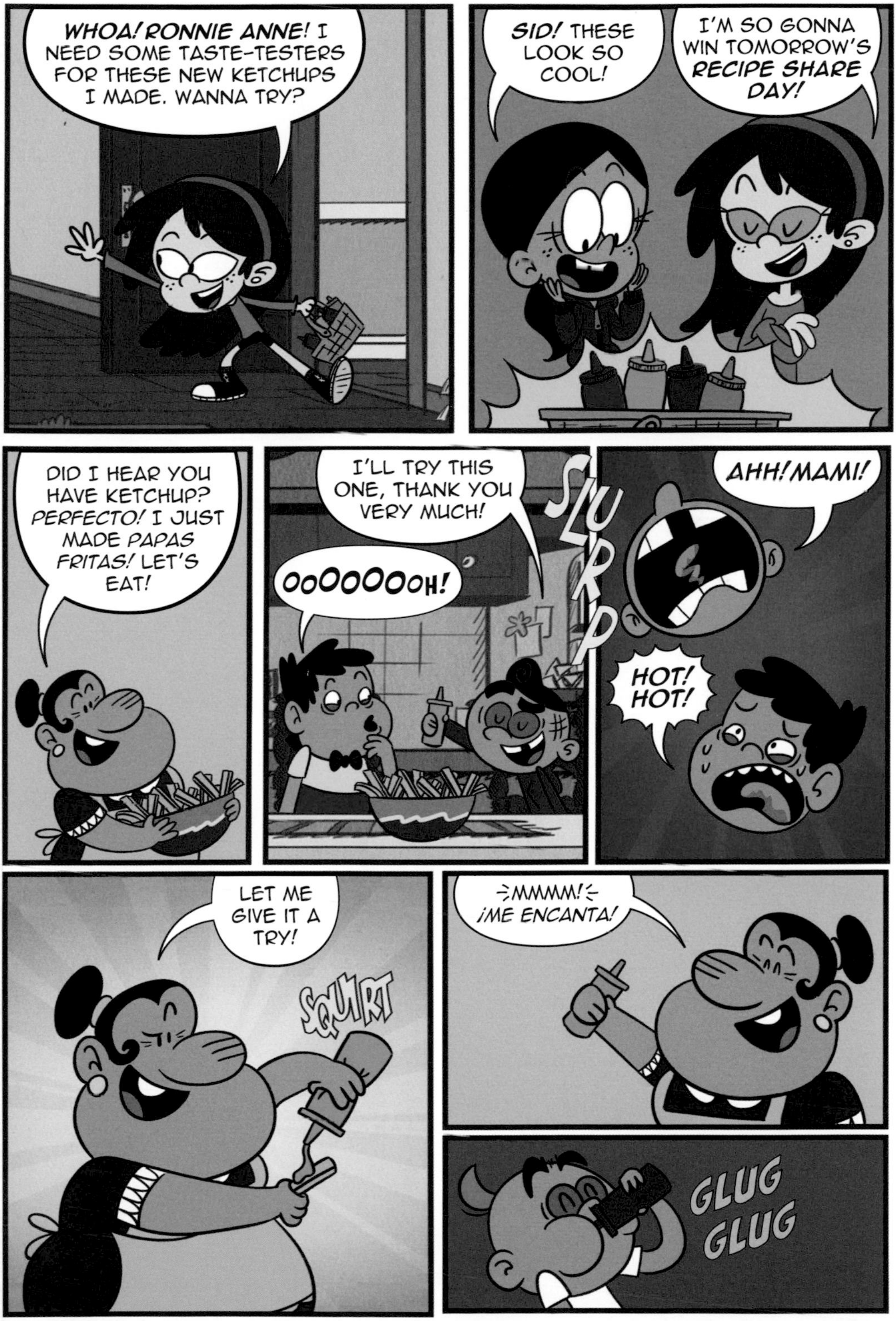
WHOA! RONNIE ANNE! I NEED SOME TASTE-TESTERS FOR THESE NEW KETCHUPS I MADE. WANNA TRY?
SID! THESE LOOK SO COOL!
I'M SO GONNA WIN TOMORROW'S RECIPE SHARE DAY!
DID I HEAR YOU HAVE KETCHUP? PERFECTO! I JUST MADE PAPAS FRITAS! LET'S EAT!
I'LL TRY THIS ONE, THANK YOU VERY MUCH!
OOOOOOOH!
SLURP
AHH! MAMI!
HOT! HOT!
LET ME GIVE IT A TRY!
SQUIRT
MMMM! ¡ME ENCANTA!
GLUG GLUG

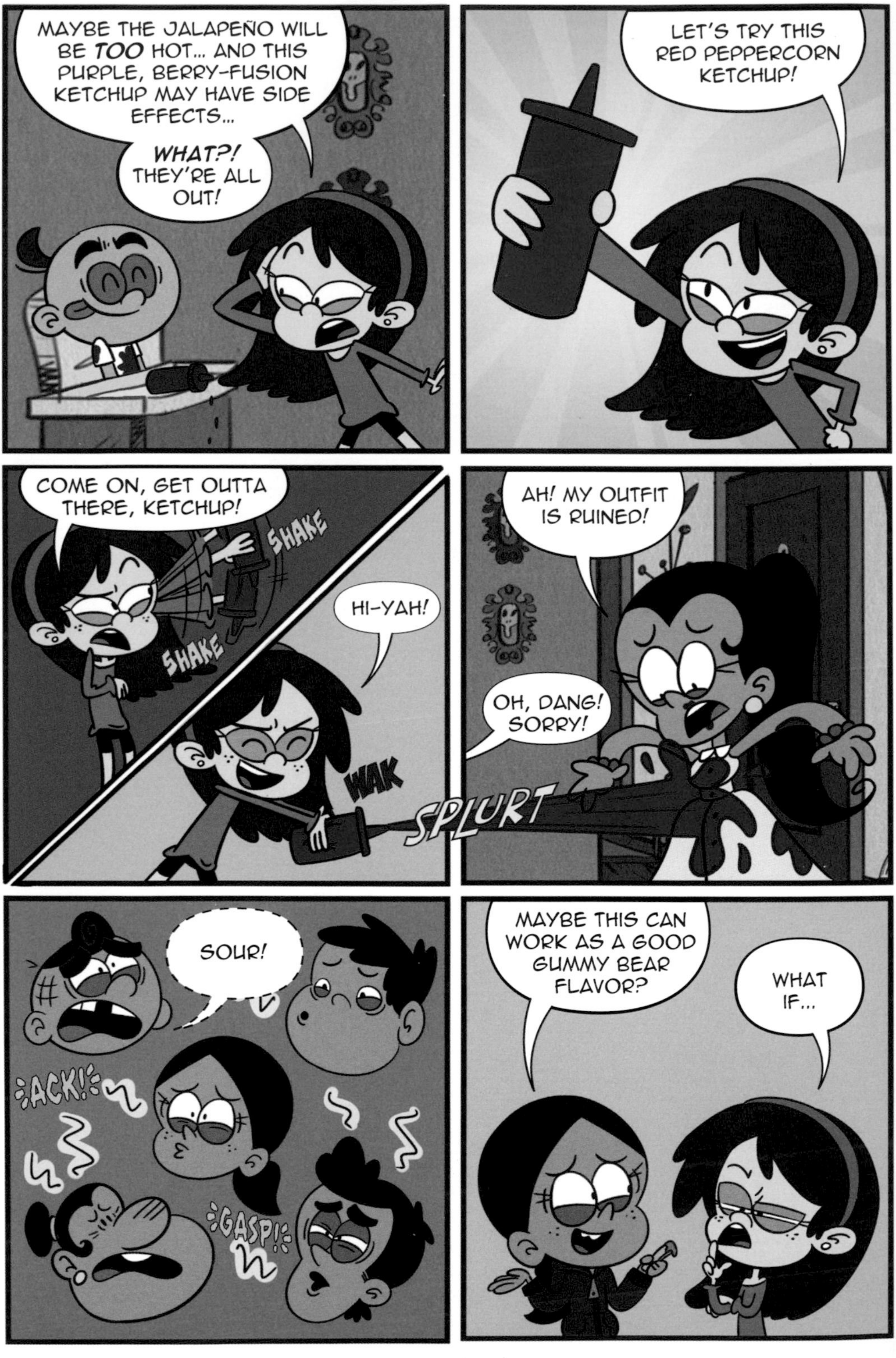
MAYBE THE JALAPEÑO WILL BE *TOO* HOT... AND THIS PURPLE, BERRY-FUSION KETCHUP MAY HAVE SIDE EFFECTS...
WHAT?! THEY'RE ALL OUT!
LET'S TRY THIS RED PEPPERCORN KETCHUP!
COME ON, GET OUTTA THERE, KETCHUP!
SHAKE
SHAKE
HI-YAH!
WAK
SPLURT
AH! MY OUTFIT IS RUINED!
OH, DANG! SORRY!
SOUR!
ACK!
GASP!
MAYBE THIS CAN WORK AS A GOOD GUMMY BEAR FLAVOR?
WHAT IF...

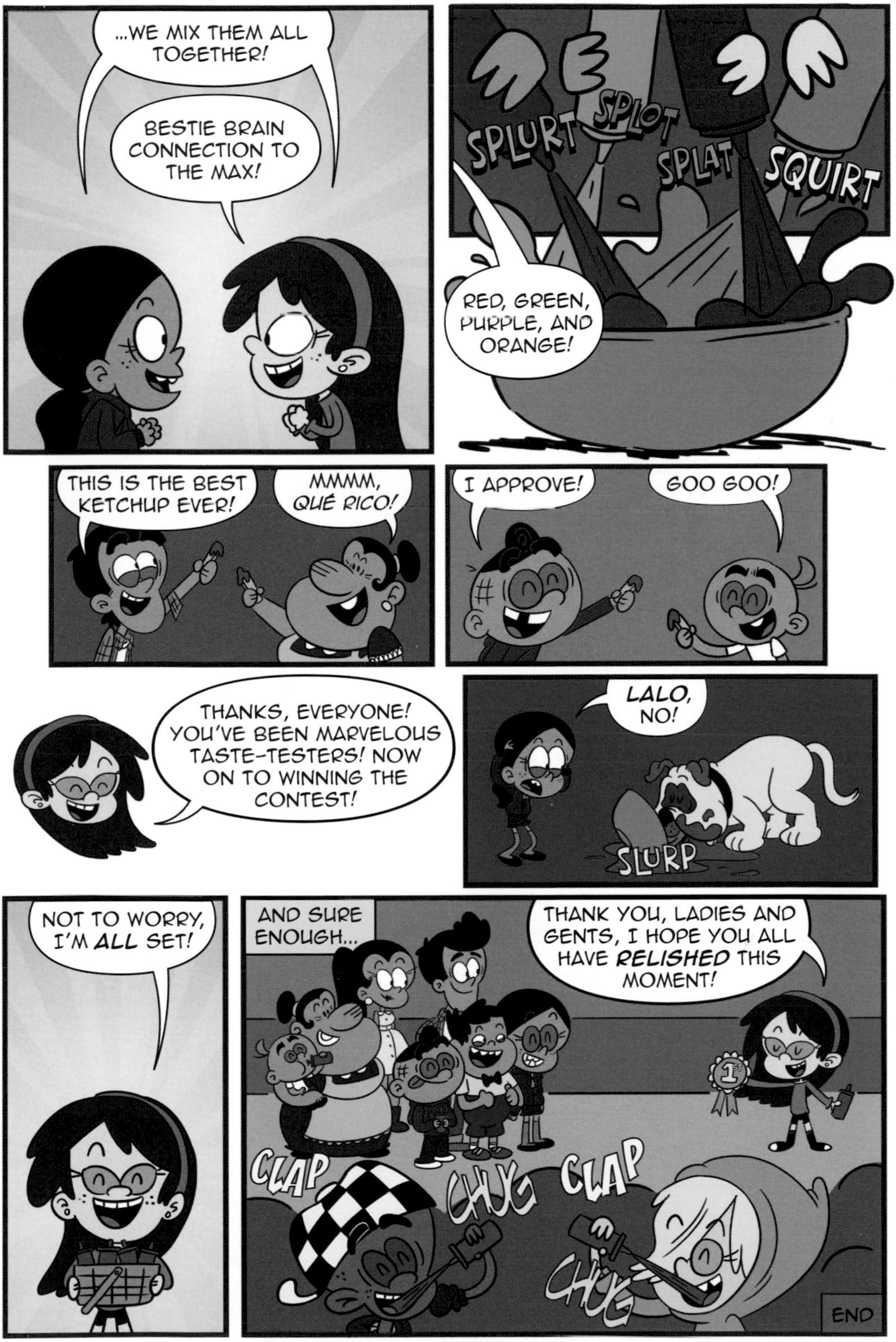
...WE MIX THEM ALL TOGETHER!
BESTIE BRAIN CONNECTION TO THE MAX!
SPLURT
SPLOT
SPLAT
SQUIRT
RED, GREEN, PURPLE, AND ORANGE!
THIS IS THE BEST KETCHUP EVER!
MMMM, QUÉ RICO!
I APPROVE!
GOO GOO!
THANKS, EVERYONE! YOU'VE BEEN MARVELOUS TASTE-TESTERS! NOW ON TO WINNING THE CONTEST!
LALO, NO!
SLURP
NOT TO WORRY, I'M ALL SET!
AND SURE ENOUGH...
THANK YOU, LADIES AND GENTS, I HOPE YOU ALL HAVE RELISHED THIS MOMENT!
1ST
CLAP
CHUG
CLAP
CHUG
END

"A GLITTERING RECIPE"

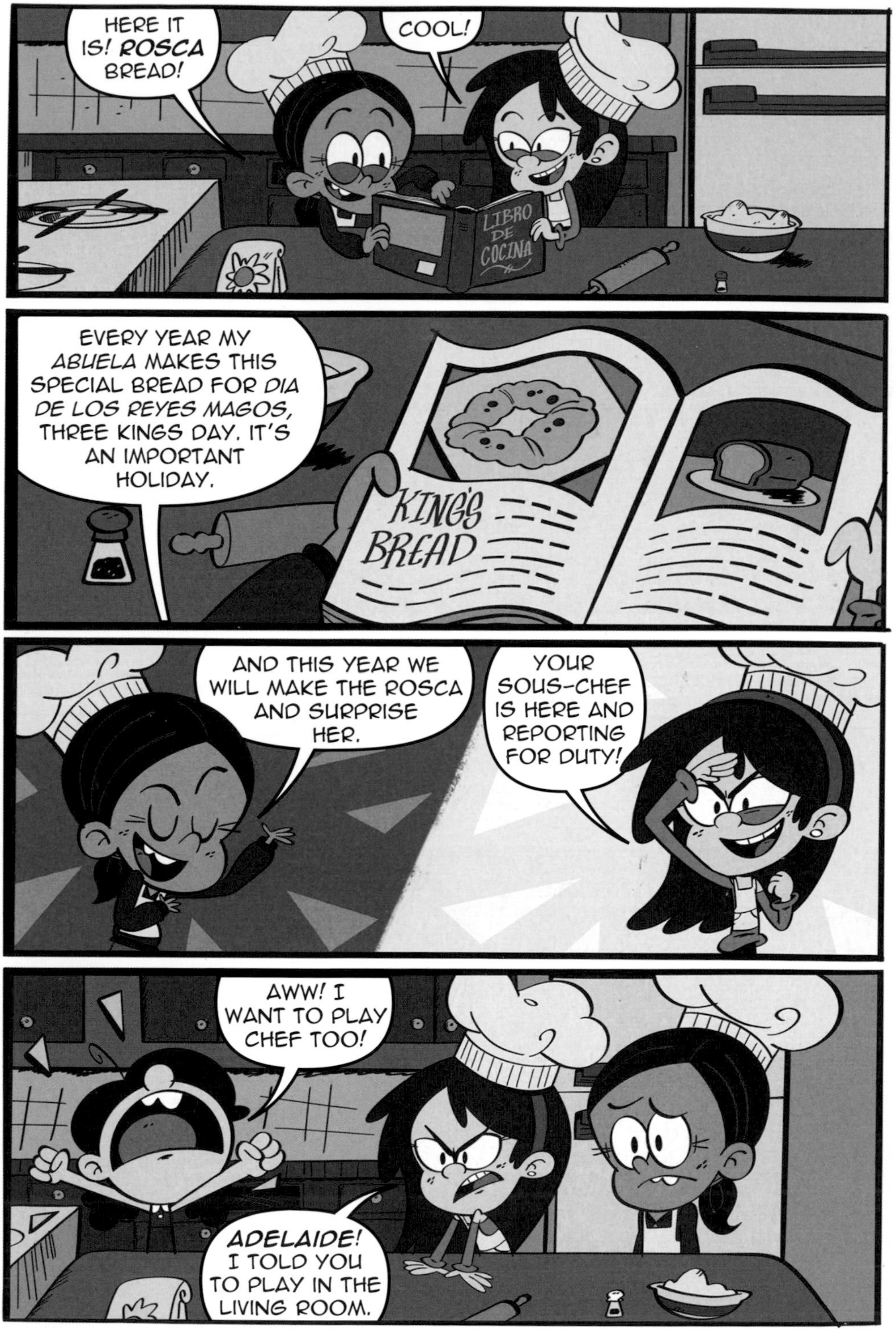
HERE IT IS! *ROSCA* BREAD!
COOL!
LIBRO DE COCINA
EVERY YEAR MY *ABUELA* MAKES THIS SPECIAL BREAD FOR *DIA DE LOS REYES MAGOS*, THREE KINGS DAY. IT'S AN IMPORTANT HOLIDAY.
KING'S BREAD
AND THIS YEAR WE WILL MAKE THE ROSCA AND SURPRISE HER.
YOUR SOUS-CHEF IS HERE AND REPORTING FOR DUTY!
AWW! I WANT TO PLAY CHEF TOO!
ADELAIDE! I TOLD YOU TO PLAY IN THE LIVING ROOM.

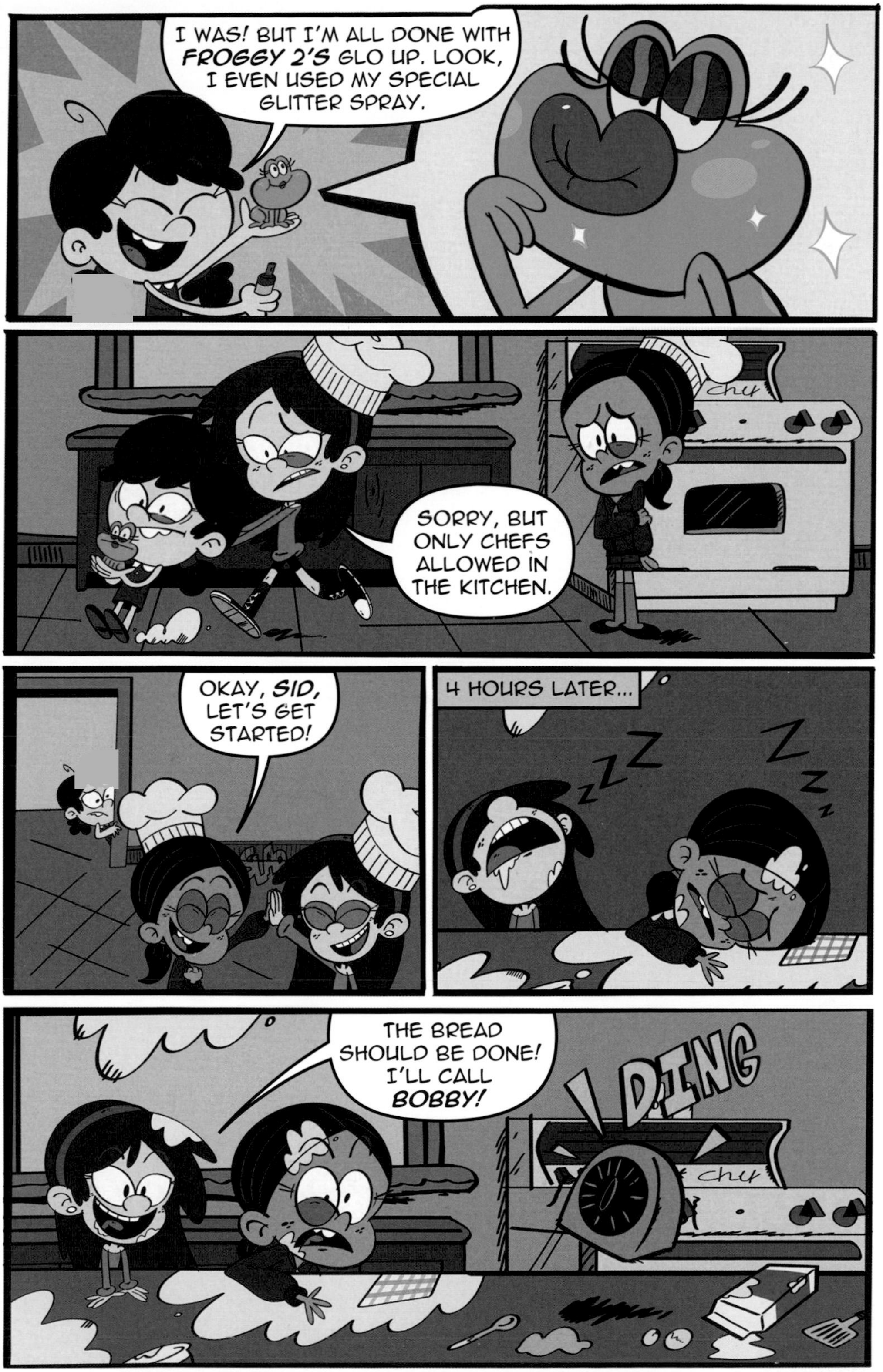
I WAS! BUT I'M ALL DONE WITH FROGGY 2'S GLO UP. LOOK, I EVEN USED MY SPECIAL GLITTER SPRAY.
SORRY, BUT ONLY CHEFS ALLOWED IN THE KITCHEN.
OKAY, SID, LET'S GET STARTED!
4 HOURS LATER...
ZZZ
ZZZ
THE BREAD SHOULD BE DONE! I'LL CALL BOBBY!
DING

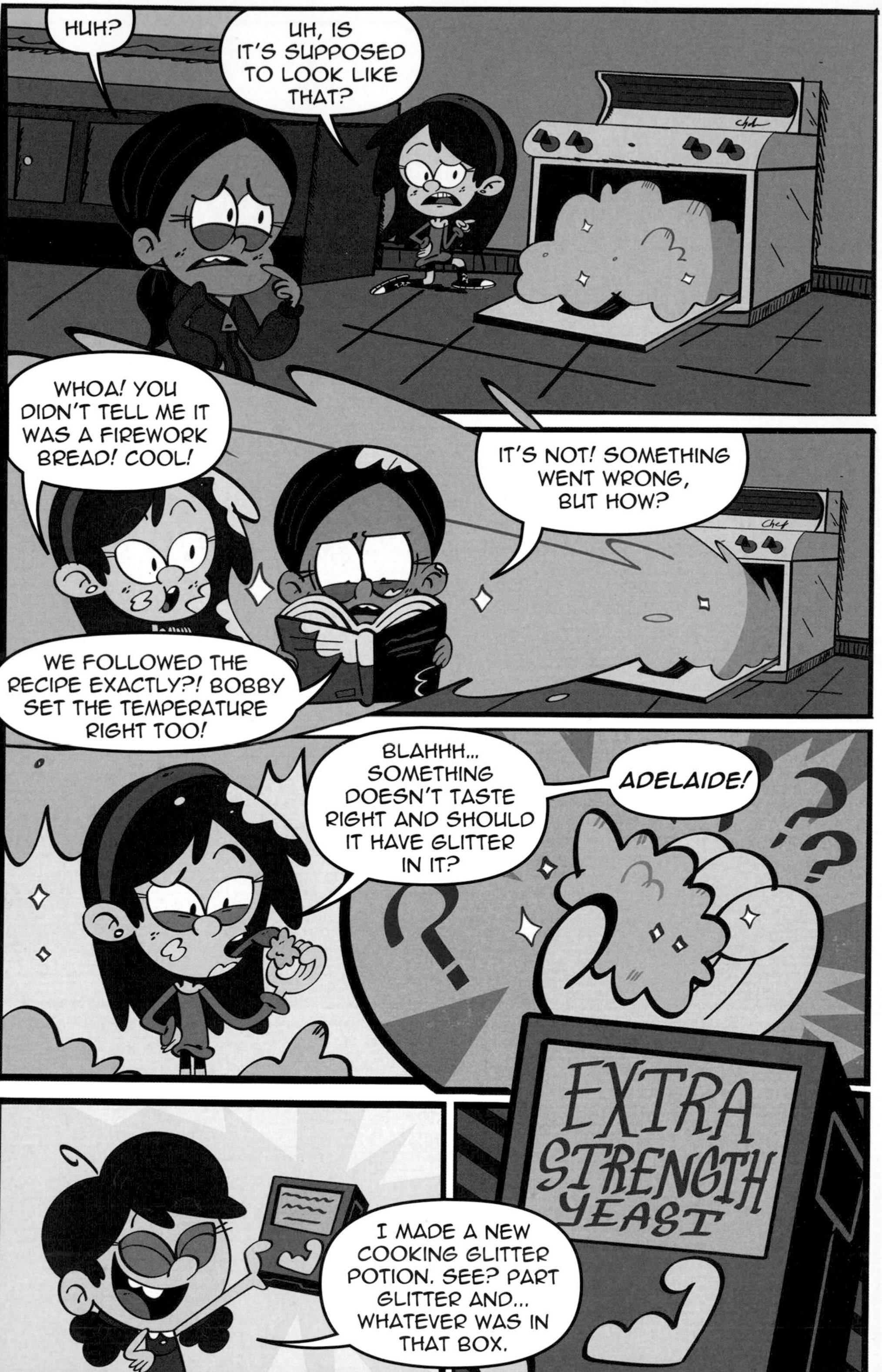
HUH?
UH, IS IT'S SUPPOSED TO LOOK LIKE THAT?
WHOA! YOU DIDN'T TELL ME IT WAS A FIREWORK BREAD! COOL!
IT'S NOT! SOMETHING WENT WRONG, BUT HOW?
WE FOLLOWED THE RECIPE EXACTLY?! BOBBY SET THE TEMPERATURE RIGHT TOO!
BLAHHH... SOMETHING DOESN'T TASTE RIGHT AND SHOULD IT HAVE GLITTER IN IT?
ADELAIDE!
EXTRA STRENGTH YEAST
I MADE A NEW COOKING GLITTER POTION. SEE? PART GLITTER AND... WHATEVER WAS IN THAT BOX.

DON'T TRY THIS AT HOME. ALWAYS HAVE AN ADULT PRESENT TO HELP BAKE ANYTHING.

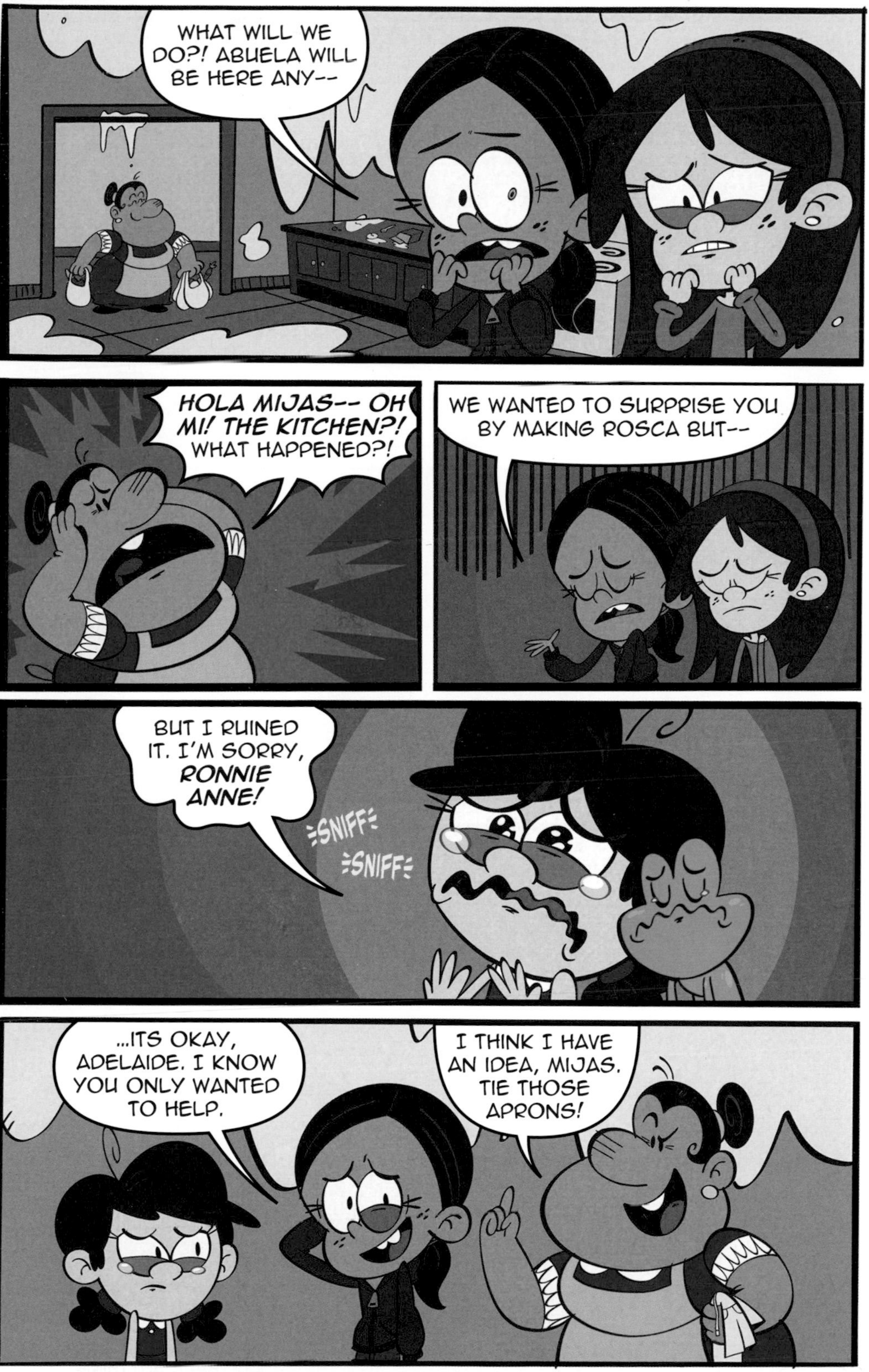
WHAT WILL WE DO?! ABUELA WILL BE HERE ANY--
HOLA MIJAS-- OH MI! THE KITCHEN?! WHAT HAPPENED?!
WE WANTED TO SURPRISE YOU BY MAKING ROSCA BUT--
BUT I RUINED IT. I'M SORRY, RONNIE ANNE!
SNIFF
SNIFF
...ITS OKAY, ADELAIDE. I KNOW YOU ONLY WANTED TO HELP.
I THINK I HAVE AN IDEA, MIJAS. TIE THOSE APRONS!

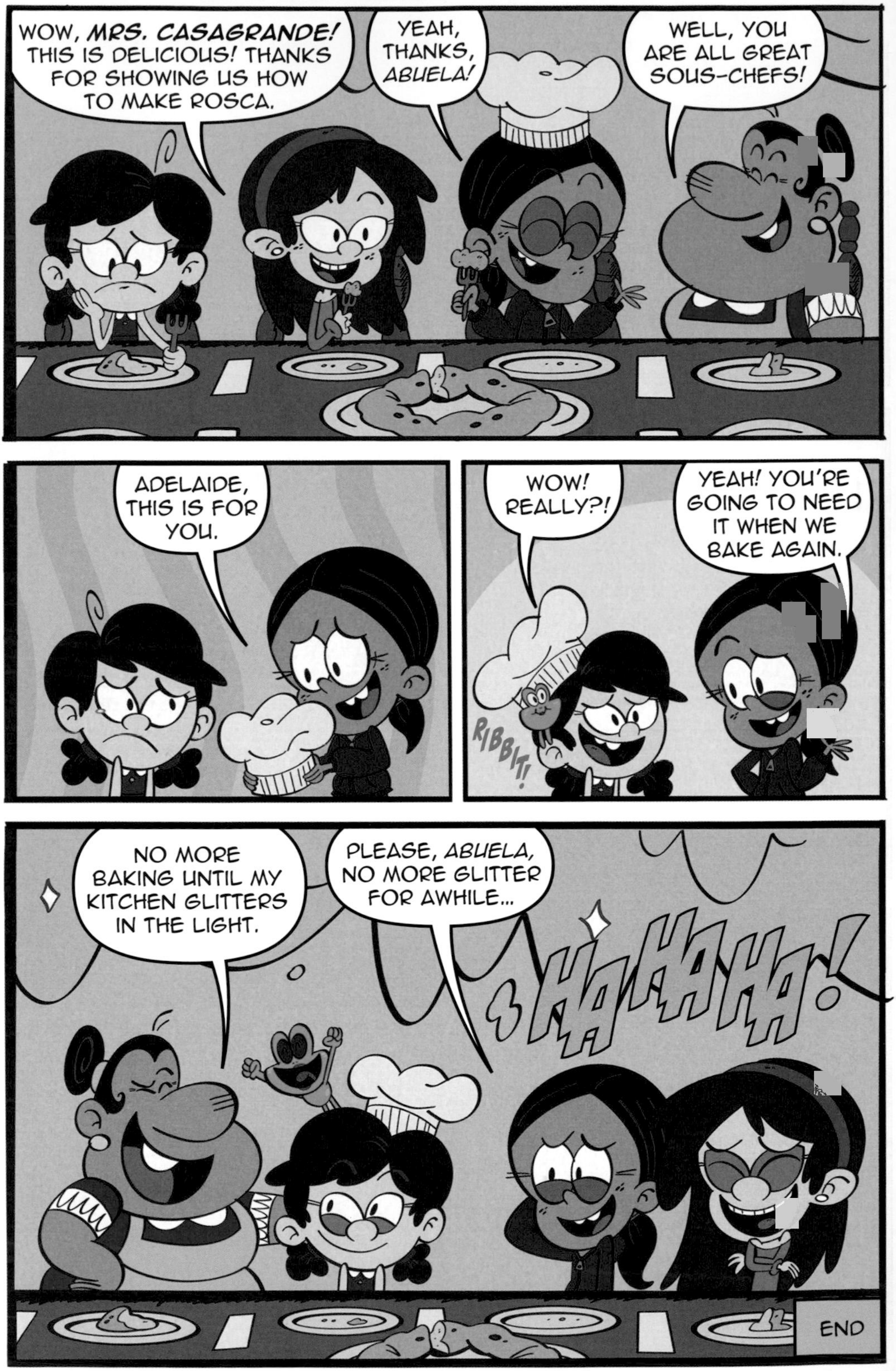

WOW, MRS. CASAGRANDE! THIS IS DELICIOUS! THANKS FOR SHOWING US HOW TO MAKE ROSCA.
YEAH, THANKS, ABUELA!
WELL, YOU ARE ALL GREAT SOUS-CHEFS!
ADELAIDE, THIS IS FOR YOU.
WOW! REALLY?!
YEAH! YOU'RE GOING TO NEED IT WHEN WE BAKE AGAIN.
RIBBIT!
NO MORE BAKING UNTIL MY KITCHEN GLITTERS IN THE LIGHT.
PLEASE, ABUELA, NO MORE GLITTER FOR AWHILE...
HAHAHAHA!
END

"COOKING WITH THE CASAGRANDES"

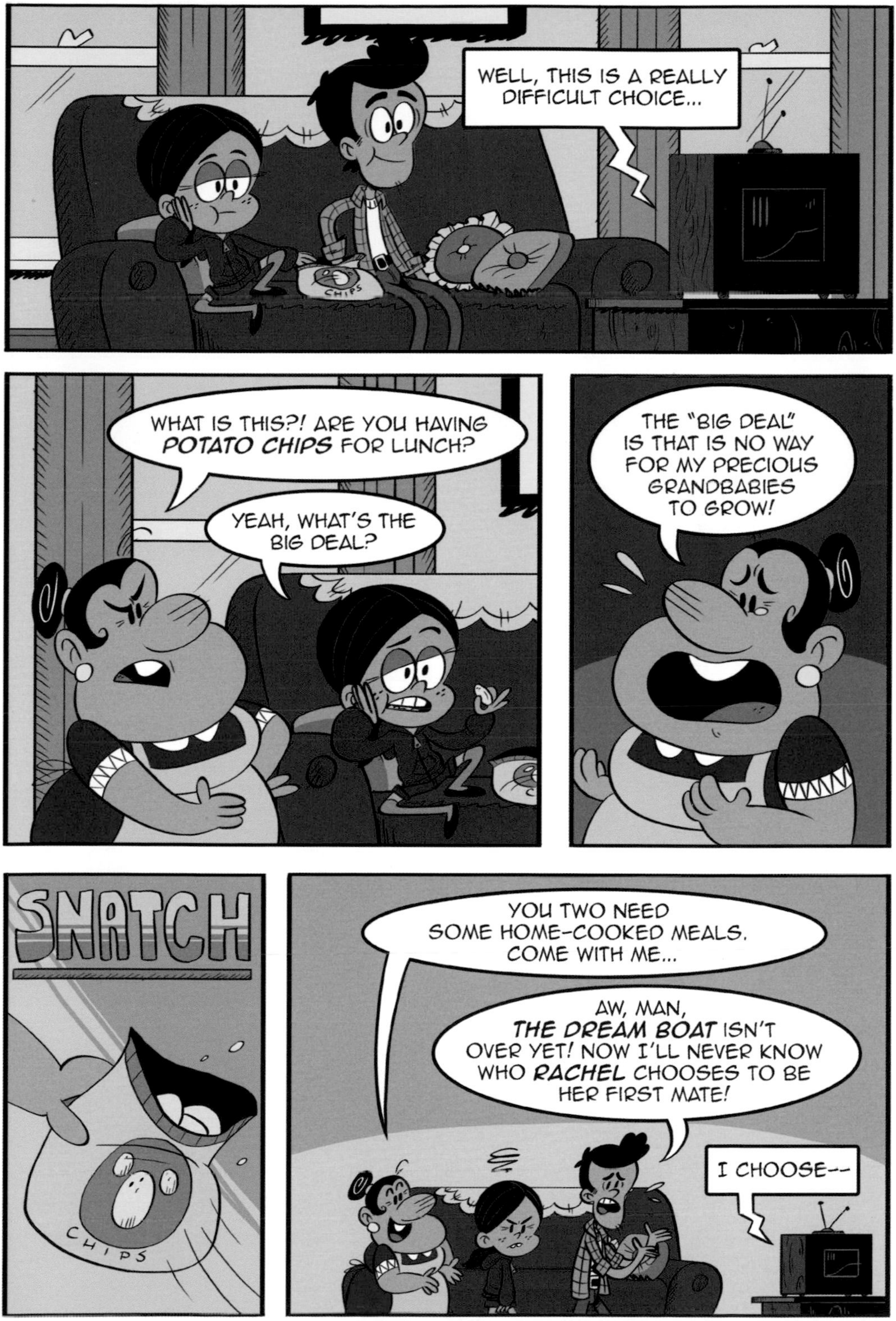

WELL, THIS IS A REALLY DIFFICULT CHOICE...
CHIPS
WHAT IS THIS?! ARE YOU HAVING *POTATO CHIPS* FOR LUNCH?
YEAH, WHAT'S THE BIG DEAL?
THE "BIG DEAL" IS THAT IS NO WAY FOR MY PRECIOUS GRANDBABIES TO GROW!
SNATCH
CHIPS
YOU TWO NEED SOME HOME-COOKED MEALS. COME WITH ME...
AW, MAN, ***THE DREAM BOAT*** ISN'T OVER YET! NOW I'LL NEVER KNOW WHO ***RACHEL*** CHOOSES TO BE HER FIRST MATE!
I CHOOSE--

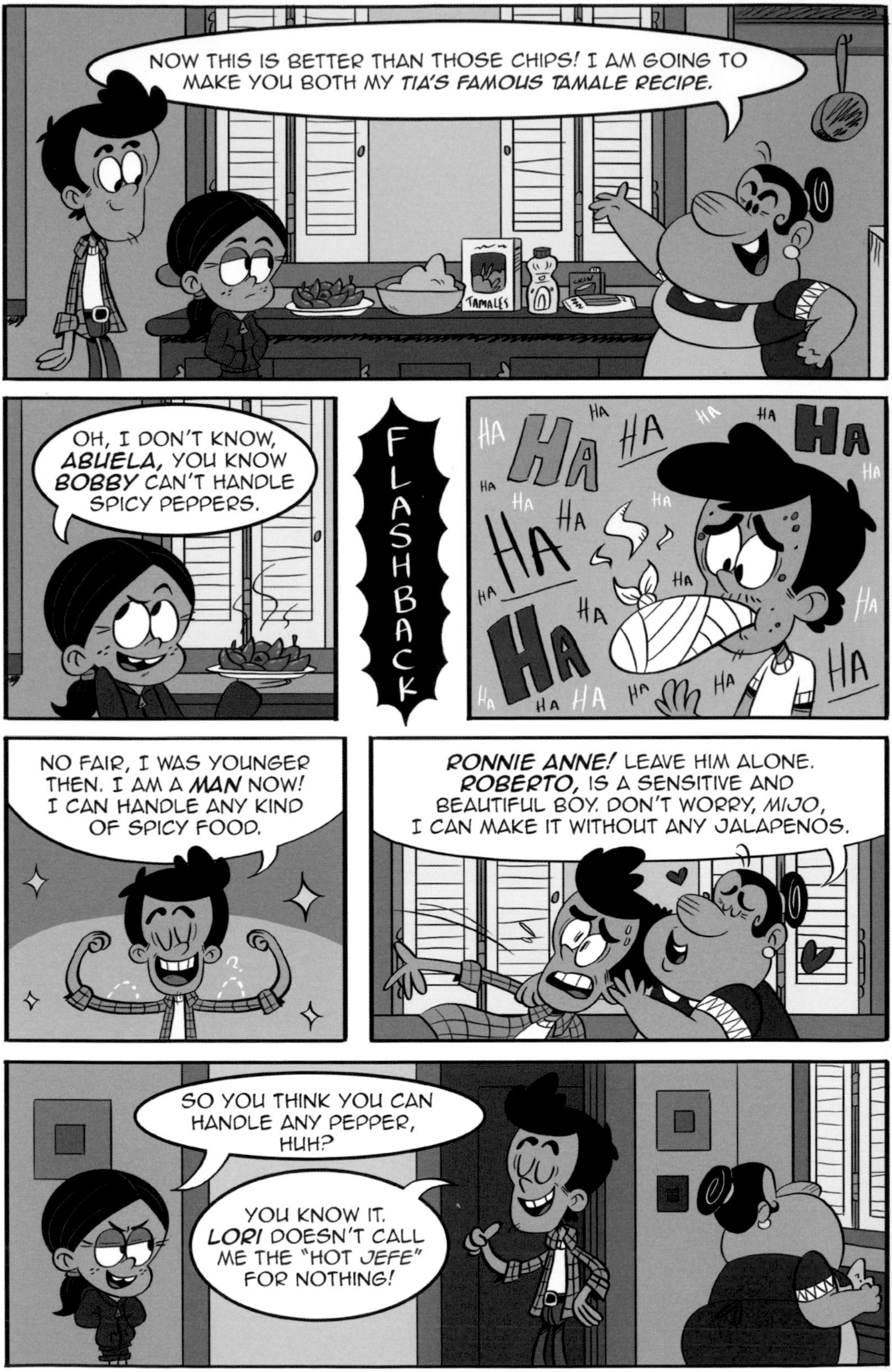
NOW THIS IS BETTER THAN THOSE CHIPS! I AM GOING TO MAKE YOU BOTH MY TIA'S FAMOUS TAMALE RECIPE.
TAMALES
OH, I DON'T KNOW, ABUELA, YOU KNOW BOBBY CAN'T HANDLE SPICY PEPPERS.
FLASHBACK
HA HA HA HA HA HA HA HA HA HA HA HA HA HA HA HA HA HA HA HA HA HA HA
NO FAIR, I WAS YOUNGER THEN. I AM A MAN NOW! I CAN HANDLE ANY KIND OF SPICY FOOD.
RONNIE ANNE! LEAVE HIM ALONE. ROBERTO, IS A SENSITIVE AND BEAUTIFUL BOY. DON'T WORRY, MIJO, I CAN MAKE IT WITHOUT ANY JALAPENOS.
SO YOU THINK YOU CAN HANDLE ANY PEPPER, HUH?
YOU KNOW IT. LORI DOESN'T CALL ME THE "HOT JEFE" FOR NOTHING!

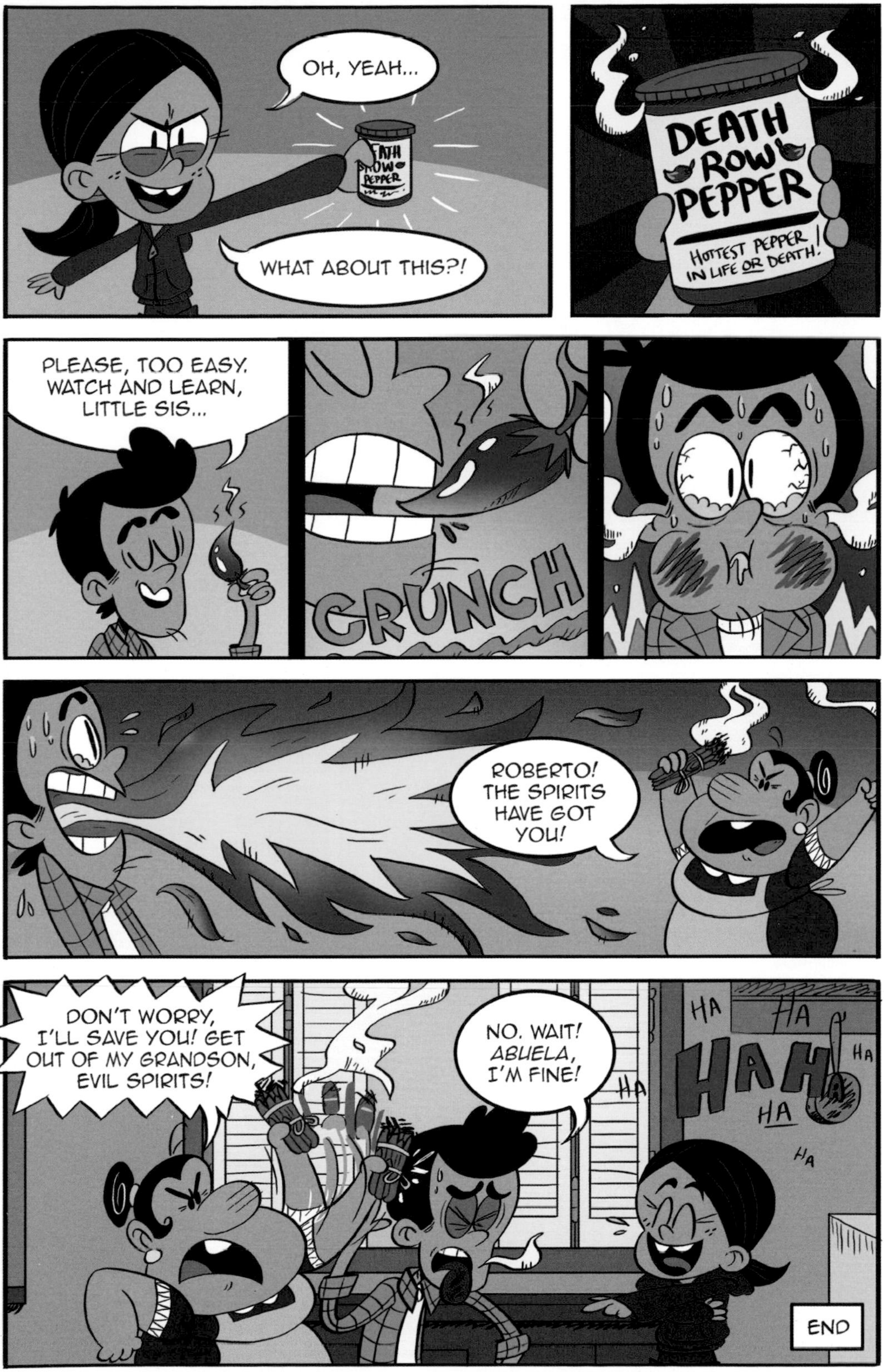
OH, YEAH...
WHAT ABOUT THIS?!
DEATH ROW PEPPER
HOTTEST PEPPER IN LIFE OR DEATH!
PLEASE, TOO EASY. WATCH AND LEARN, LITTLE SIS...
CRUNCH
ROBERTO! THE SPIRITS HAVE GOT YOU!
DON'T WORRY, I'LL SAVE YOU! GET OUT OF MY GRANDSON, EVIL SPIRITS!
NO. WAIT! ABUELA, I'M FINE!
HA HA HAH HA HA HA HA HA
END

"SNACK ATTACK"

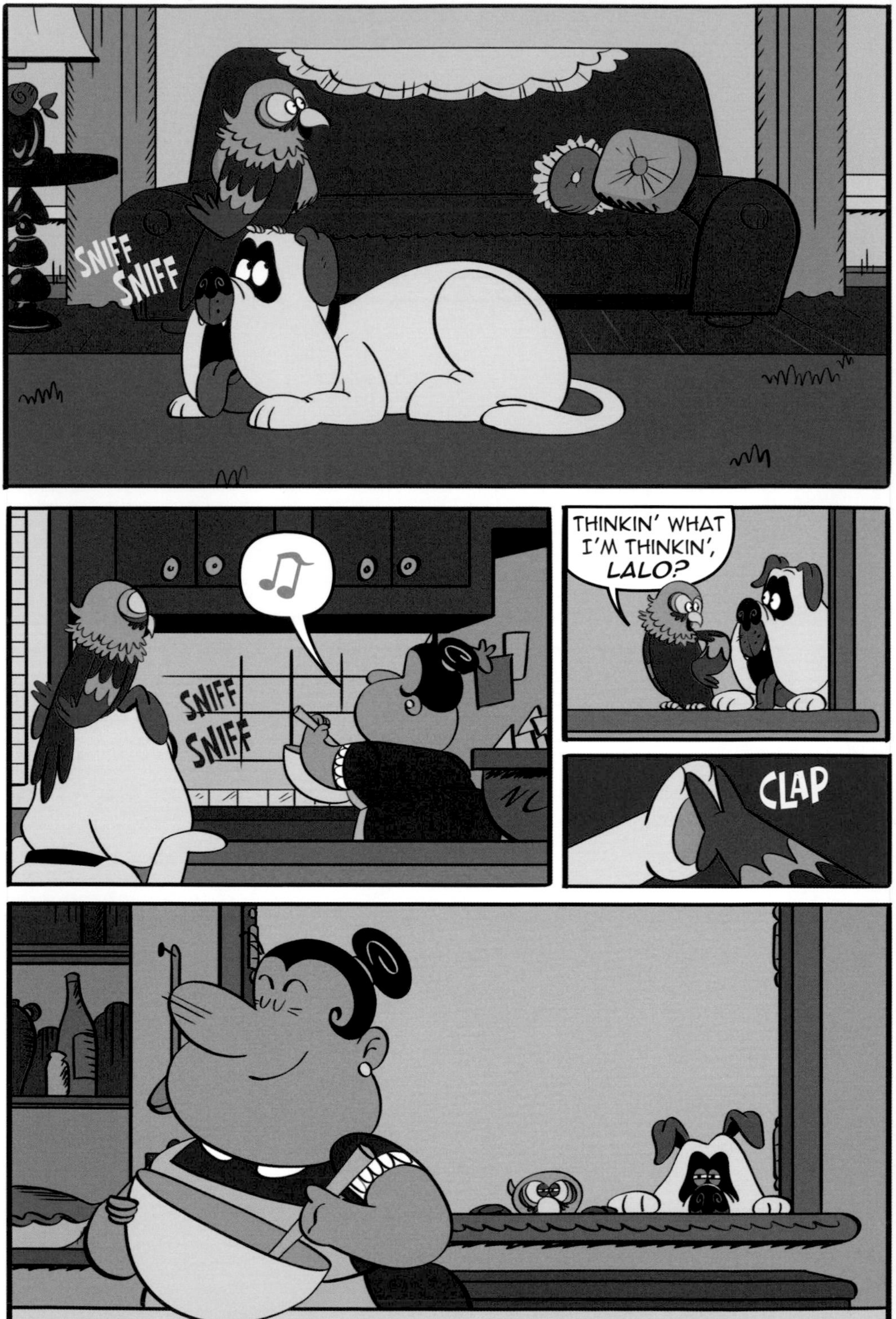
SNIFF SNIFF
SNIFF SNIFF
♫
THINKIN' WHAT I'M THINKIN', LALO?
CLAP

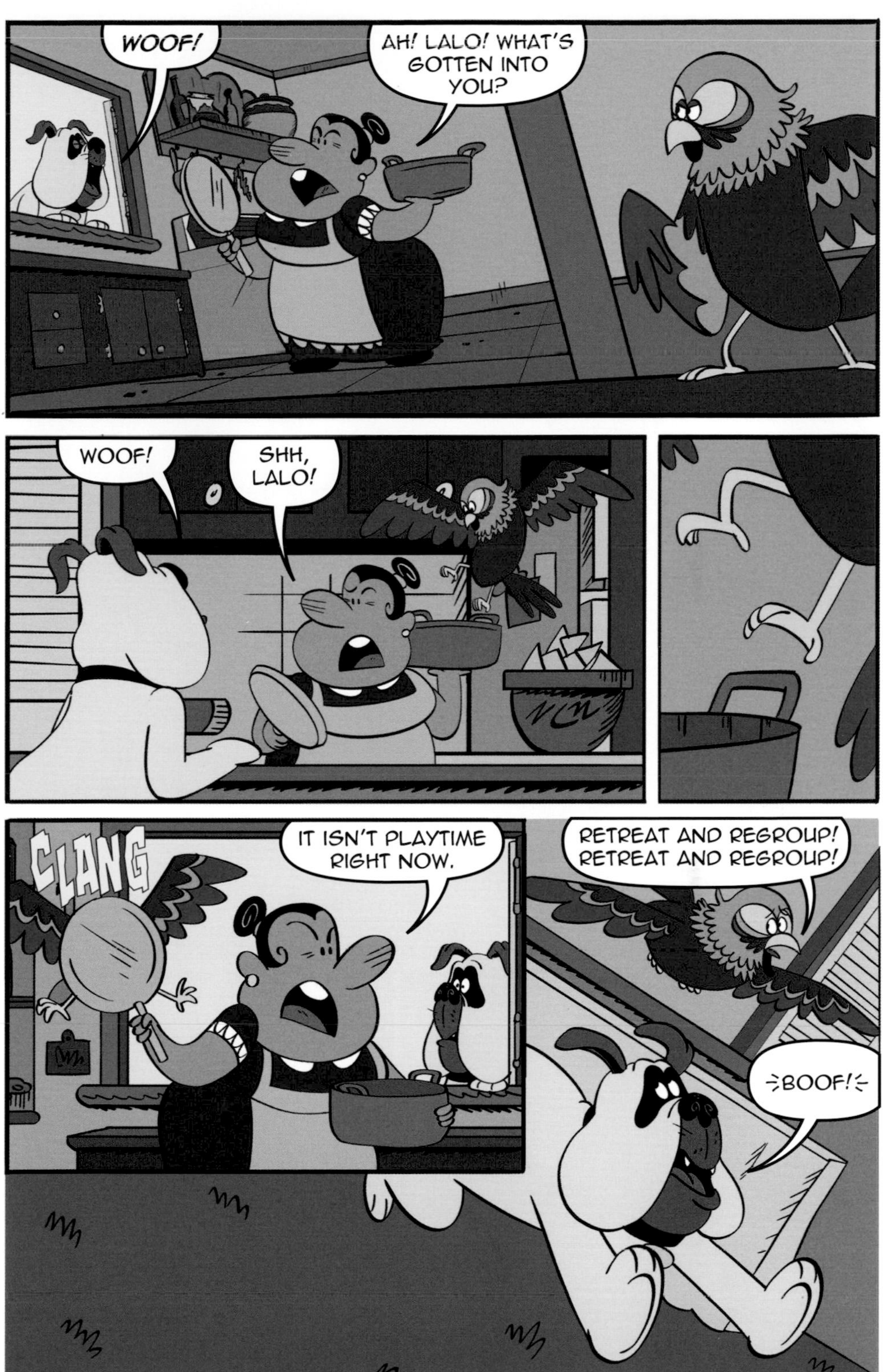
WOOF!
AH! LALO! WHAT'S GOTTEN INTO YOU?
WOOF!
SHH, LALO!
CLANG
IT ISN'T PLAYTIME RIGHT NOW.
RETREAT AND REGROUP! RETREAT AND REGROUP!
BOOF!

=BRAWK!= LOOKIN' GOOD!

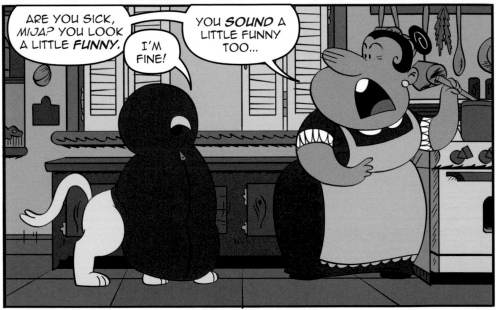
ARE YOU SICK, MIJA? YOU LOOK A LITTLE *FUNNY*.

I'M FINE!

YOU *SOUND* A LITTLE FUNNY TOO...

SERGIO?

=ACK!=

OUT WITH THE BOTH OF YOU!

LET ME COOK IN PEACE!

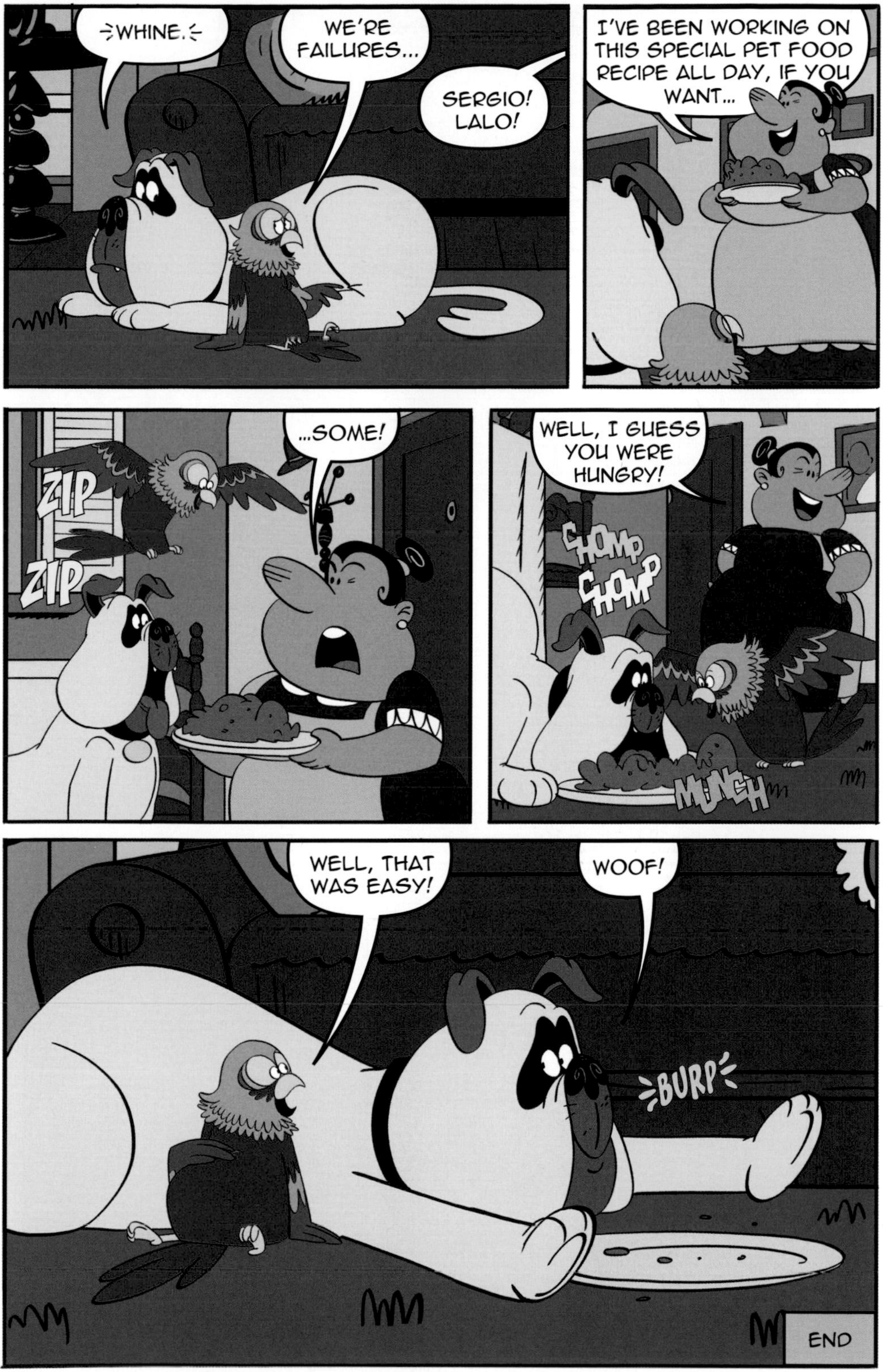

WHINE.
WE'RE FAILURES...
SERGIO! LALO!
I'VE BEEN WORKING ON THIS SPECIAL PET FOOD RECIPE ALL DAY, IF YOU WANT...
ZIP
ZIP
...SOME!
WELL, I GUESS YOU WERE HUNGRY!
CHOMP
CHOMP
MUNCH
WELL, THAT WAS EASY!
WOOF!
BURP
END

"MISSION IMPAWSIBLE"

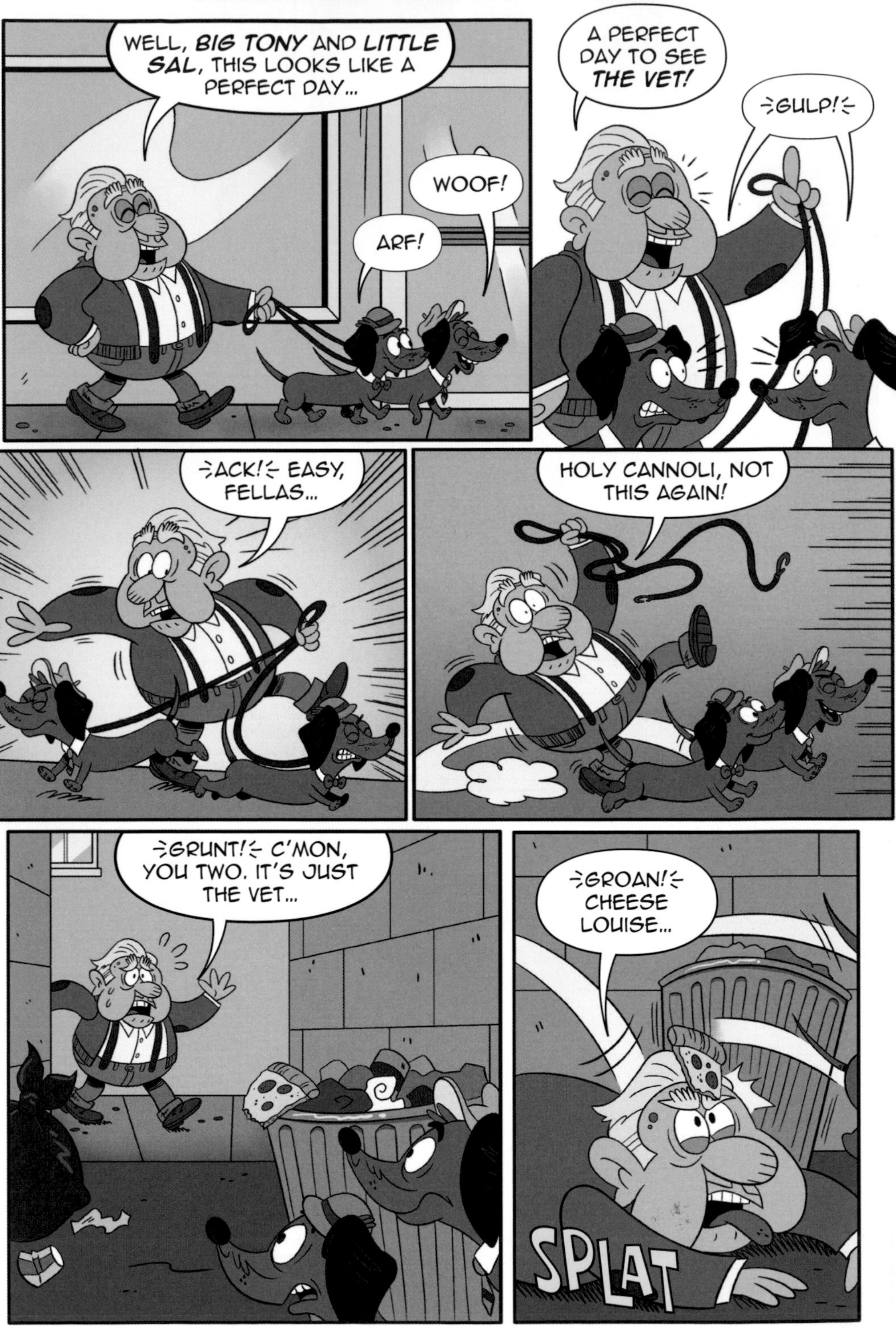

WELL, BIG TONY AND LITTLE SAL, THIS LOOKS LIKE A PERFECT DAY...
WOOF!
ARF!
A PERFECT DAY TO SEE THE VET!
GULP!
ACK! EASY, FELLAS...
HOLY CANNOLI, NOT THIS AGAIN!
GRUNT! C'MON, YOU TWO. IT'S JUST THE VET...
GROAN! CHEESE LOUISE...
SPLAT

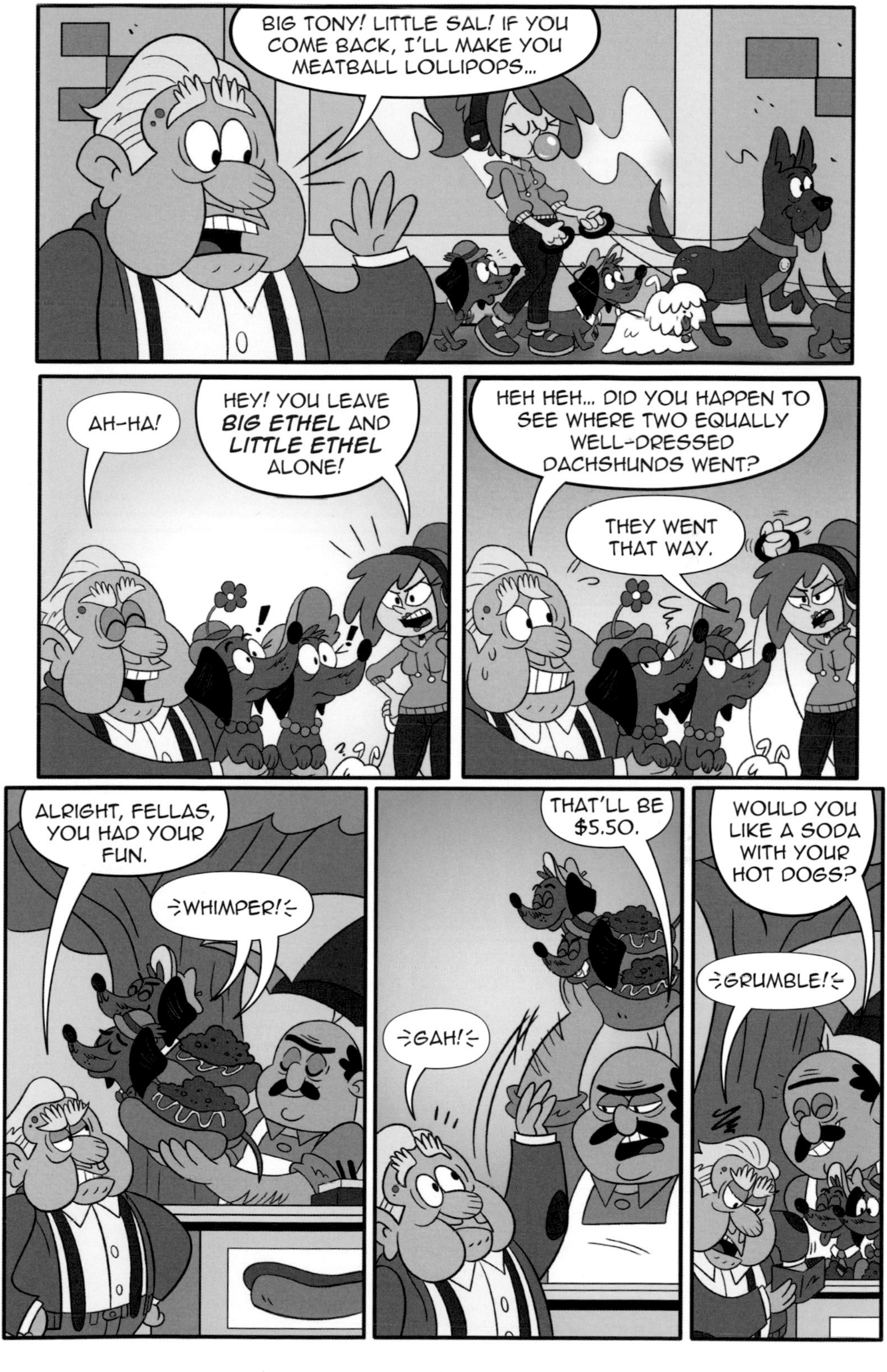
BIG TONY! LITTLE SAL! IF YOU COME BACK, I'LL MAKE YOU MEATBALL LOLLIPOPS...
AH-HA!
HEY! YOU LEAVE BIG ETHEL AND LITTLE ETHEL ALONE!
HEH HEH... DID YOU HAPPEN TO SEE WHERE TWO EQUALLY WELL-DRESSED DACHSHUNDS WENT?
THEY WENT THAT WAY.
ALRIGHT, FELLAS, YOU HAD YOUR FUN.
WHIMPER!
THAT'LL BE $5.50.
GAH!
WOULD YOU LIKE A SODA WITH YOUR HOT DOGS?
GRUMBLE!

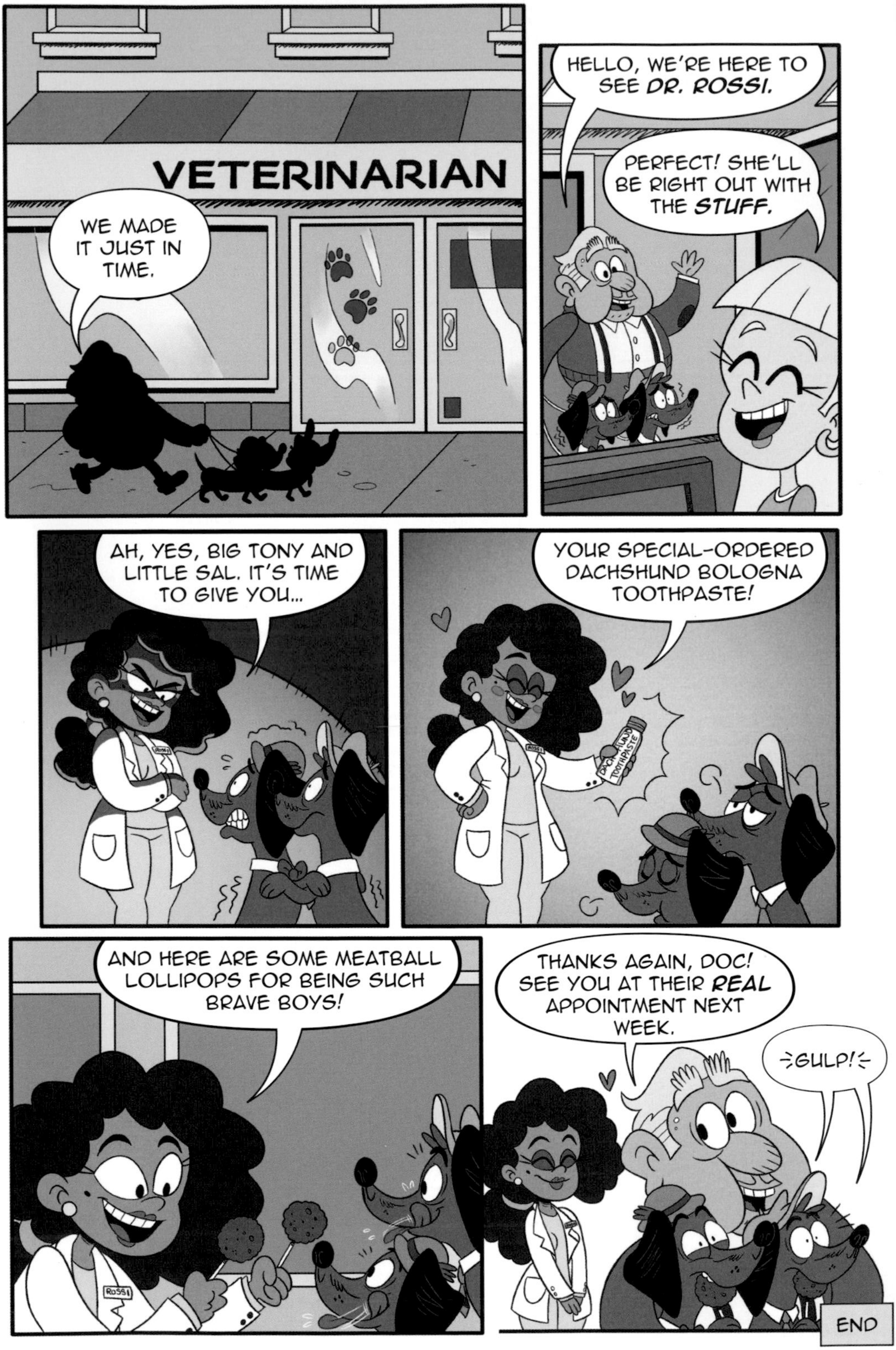
VETERINARIAN
WE MADE IT JUST IN TIME.
HELLO, WE'RE HERE TO SEE DR. ROSSI.
PERFECT! SHE'LL BE RIGHT OUT WITH THE STUFF.
AH, YES, BIG TONY AND LITTLE SAL. IT'S TIME TO GIVE YOU...
YOUR SPECIAL-ORDERED DACHSHUND BOLOGNA TOOTHPASTE!
DACHSHUND TOOTHPASTE
AND HERE ARE SOME MEATBALL LOLLIPOPS FOR BEING SUCH BRAVE BOYS!
ROSSI
THANKS AGAIN, DOC! SEE YOU AT THEIR REAL APPOINTMENT NEXT WEEK.
GULP!
END

"PARTY ANIMALS"

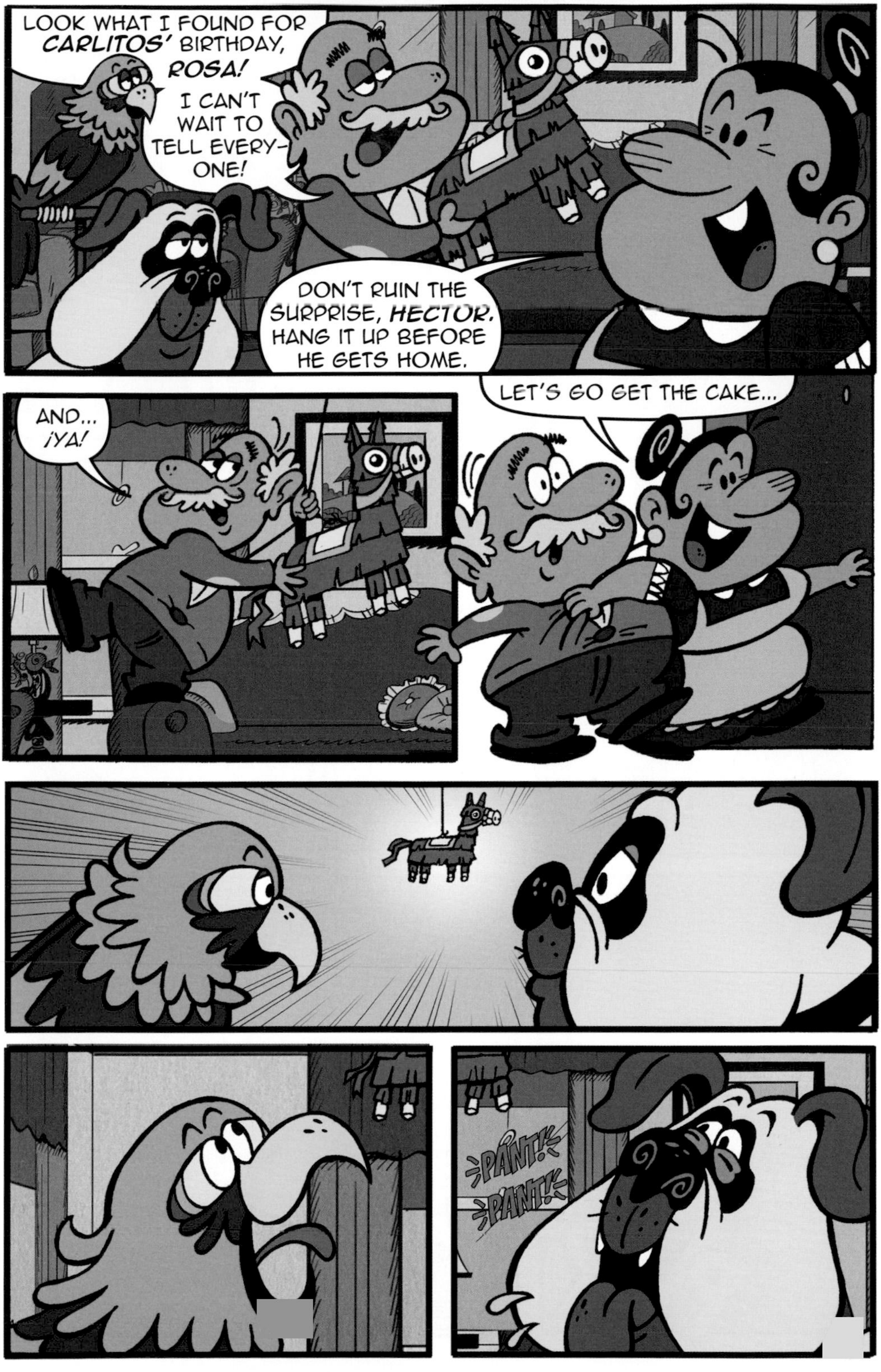
LOOK WHAT I FOUND FOR CARLITOS' BIRTHDAY, ROSA!
I CAN'T WAIT TO TELL EVERY-ONE!
DON'T RUIN THE SURPRISE, HECTOR. HANG IT UP BEFORE HE GETS HOME.
AND... ¡YA!
LET'S GO GET THE CAKE...
PANT!
PANT!

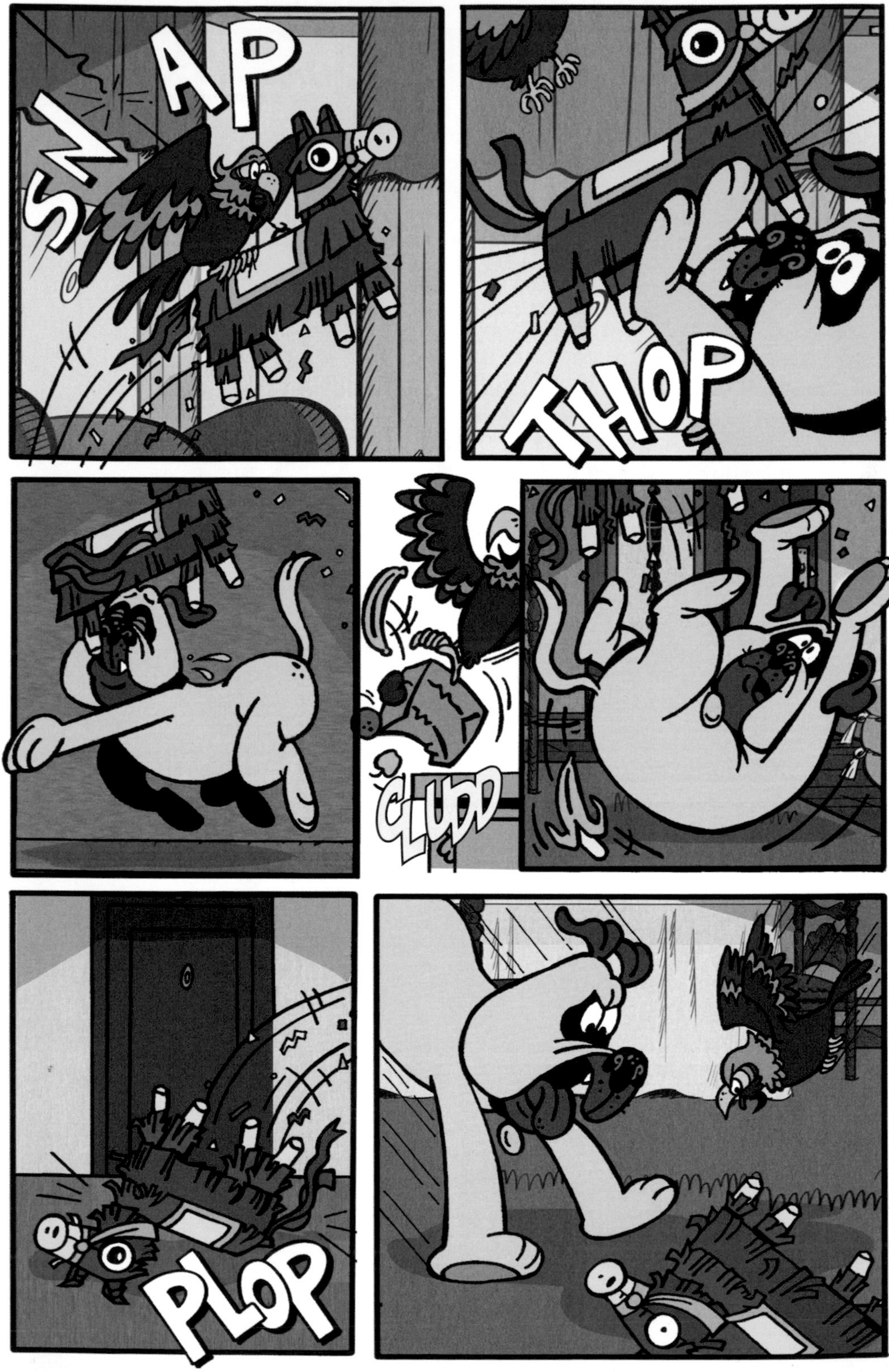
SNAP
THOP
CLUDD
PLOP

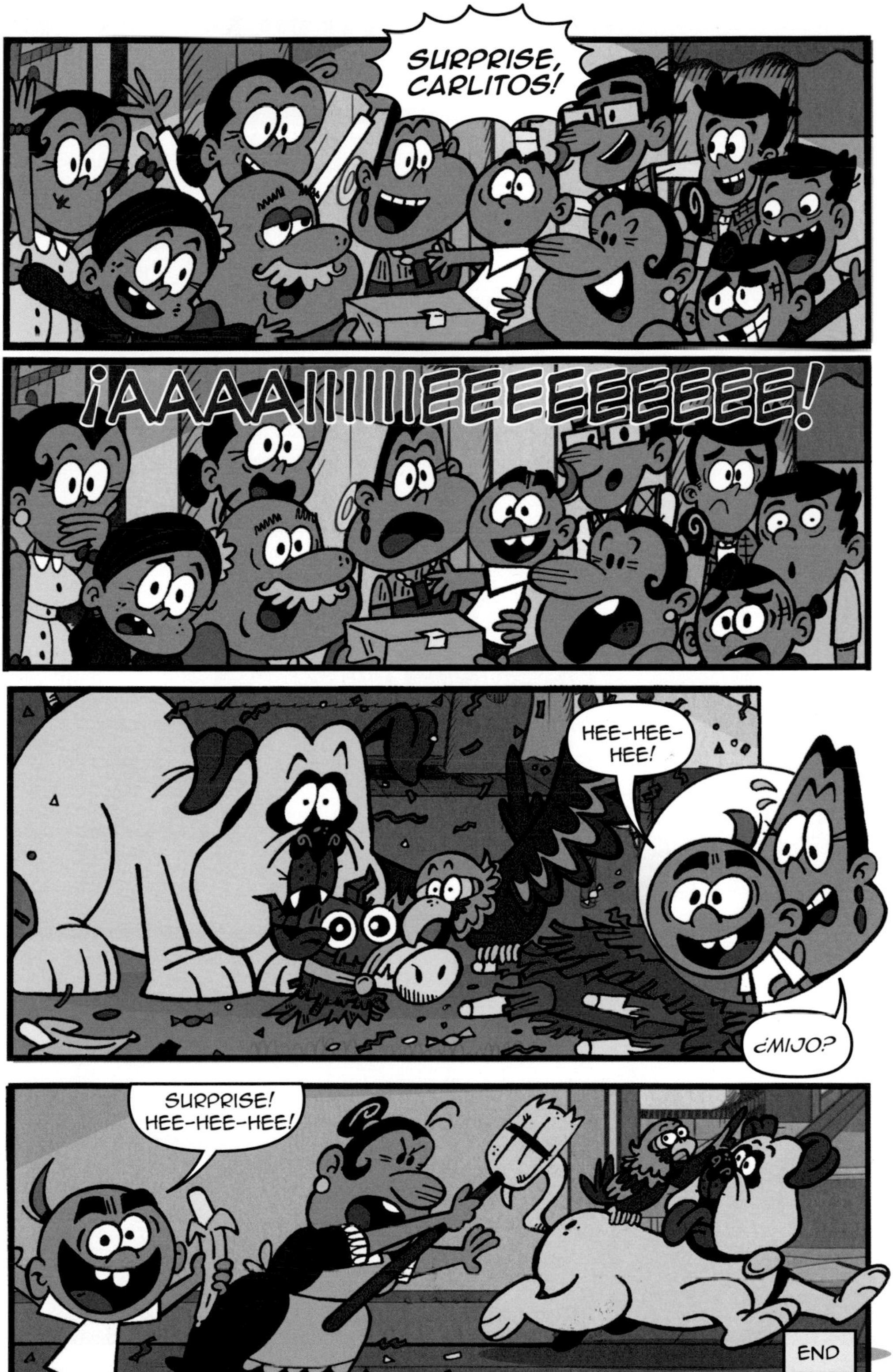
SURPRISE, CARLITOS!
¡AAAAIIIIIIEEEEEEEEEE!
HEE-HEE-HEE!
¿MIJO?
SURPRISE! HEE-HEE-HEE!
END

"COMIC RELIEF"

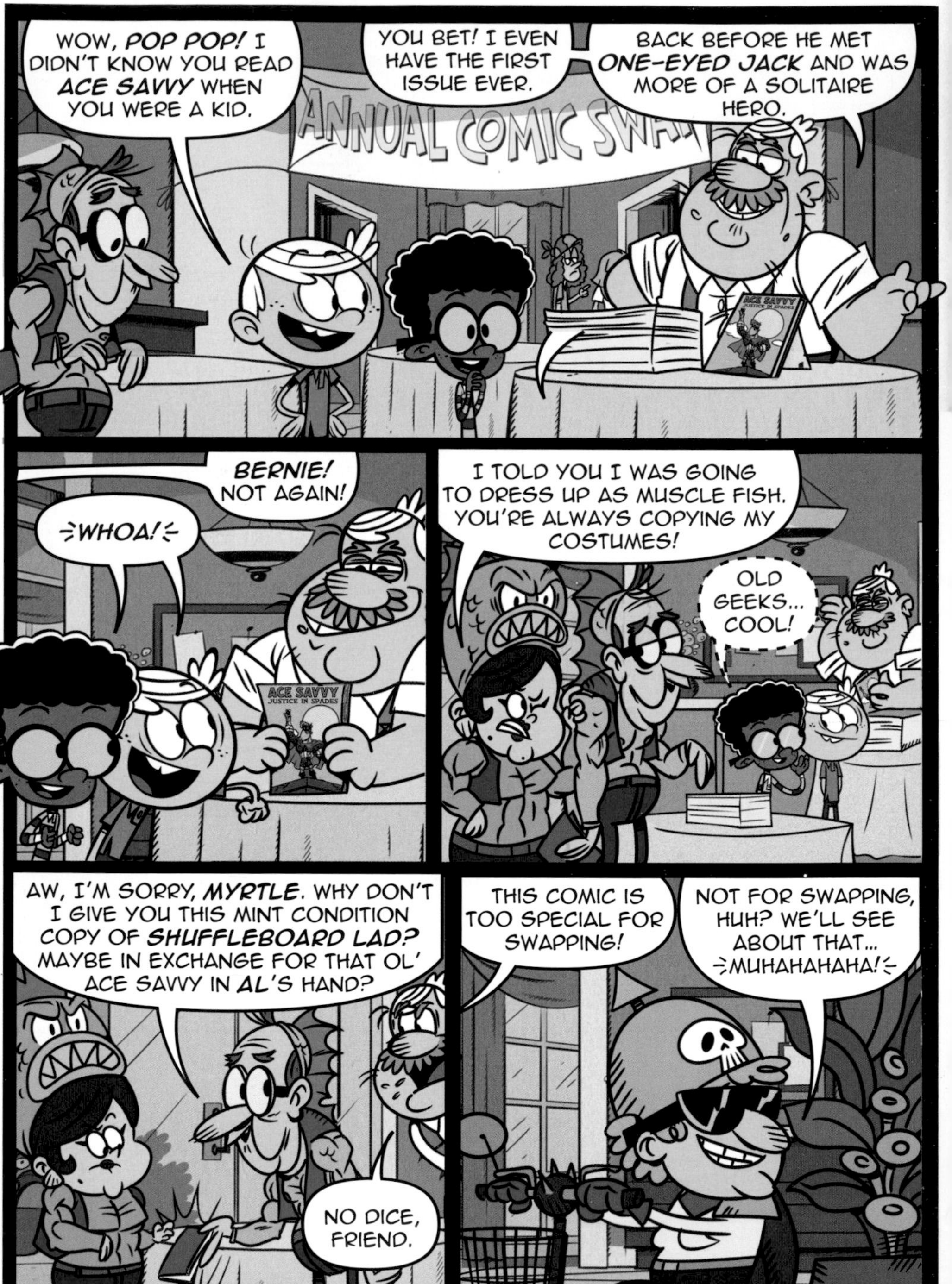
WOW, POP POP! I DIDN'T KNOW YOU READ ACE SAVVY WHEN YOU WERE A KID.
YOU BET! I EVEN HAVE THE FIRST ISSUE EVER.
BACK BEFORE HE MET ONE-EYED JACK AND WAS MORE OF A SOLITAIRE HERO.
ANNUAL COMIC SWA
ACE SAVVY JUSTICE IN SPADES
BERNIE! NOT AGAIN!
WHOA!
ACE SAVVY JUSTICE IN SPADES
I TOLD YOU I WAS GOING TO DRESS UP AS MUSCLE FISH. YOU'RE ALWAYS COPYING MY COSTUMES!
OLD GEEKS... COOL!
AW, I'M SORRY, MYRTLE. WHY DON'T I GIVE YOU THIS MINT CONDITION COPY OF SHUFFLEBOARD LAD? MAYBE IN EXCHANGE FOR THAT OL' ACE SAVVY IN AL'S HAND?
NO DICE, FRIEND.
THIS COMIC IS TOO SPECIAL FOR SWAPPING!
NOT FOR SWAPPING, HUH? WE'LL SEE ABOUT THAT... MUHAHAHAHA!

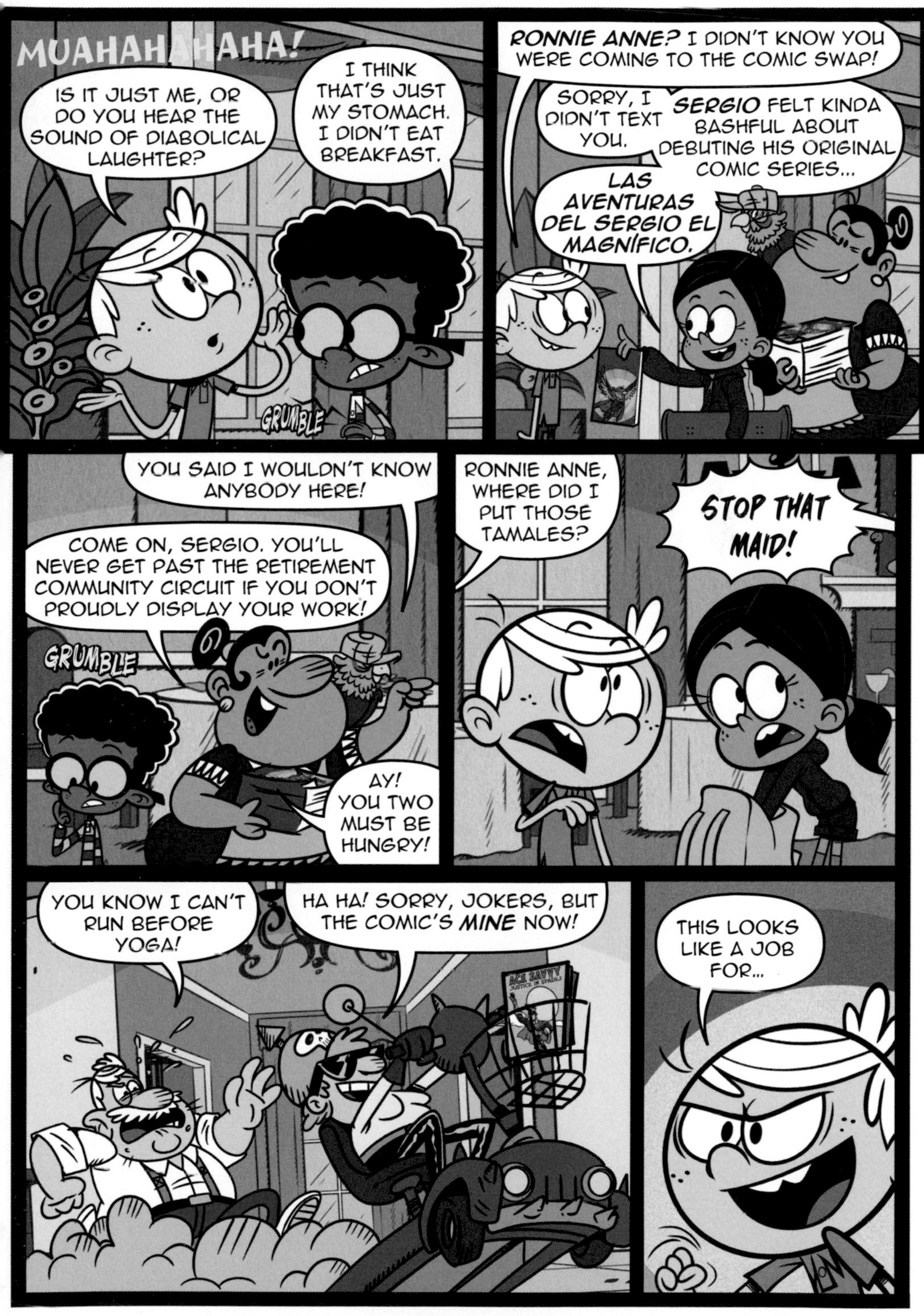
MUAHAHAHAHA!
IS IT JUST ME, OR DO YOU HEAR THE SOUND OF DIABOLICAL LAUGHTER?
I THINK THAT'S JUST MY STOMACH. I DIDN'T EAT BREAKFAST.
GRUMBLE
RONNIE ANNE? I DIDN'T KNOW YOU WERE COMING TO THE COMIC SWAP!
SORRY, I DIDN'T TEXT YOU.
SERGIO FELT KINDA BASHFUL ABOUT DEBUTING HIS ORIGINAL COMIC SERIES...
LAS AVENTURAS DEL SERGIO EL MAGNÍFICO.
YOU SAID I WOULDN'T KNOW ANYBODY HERE!
COME ON, SERGIO. YOU'LL NEVER GET PAST THE RETIREMENT COMMUNITY CIRCUIT IF YOU DON'T PROUDLY DISPLAY YOUR WORK!
GRUMBLE
AY! YOU TWO MUST BE HUNGRY!
RONNIE ANNE, WHERE DID I PUT THOSE TAMALES?
STOP THAT MAID!
YOU KNOW I CAN'T RUN BEFORE YOGA!
HA HA! SORRY, JOKERS, BUT THE COMIC'S MINE NOW!
ACE SAVVY
JUSTICE IN SPADES
THIS LOOKS LIKE A JOB FOR...

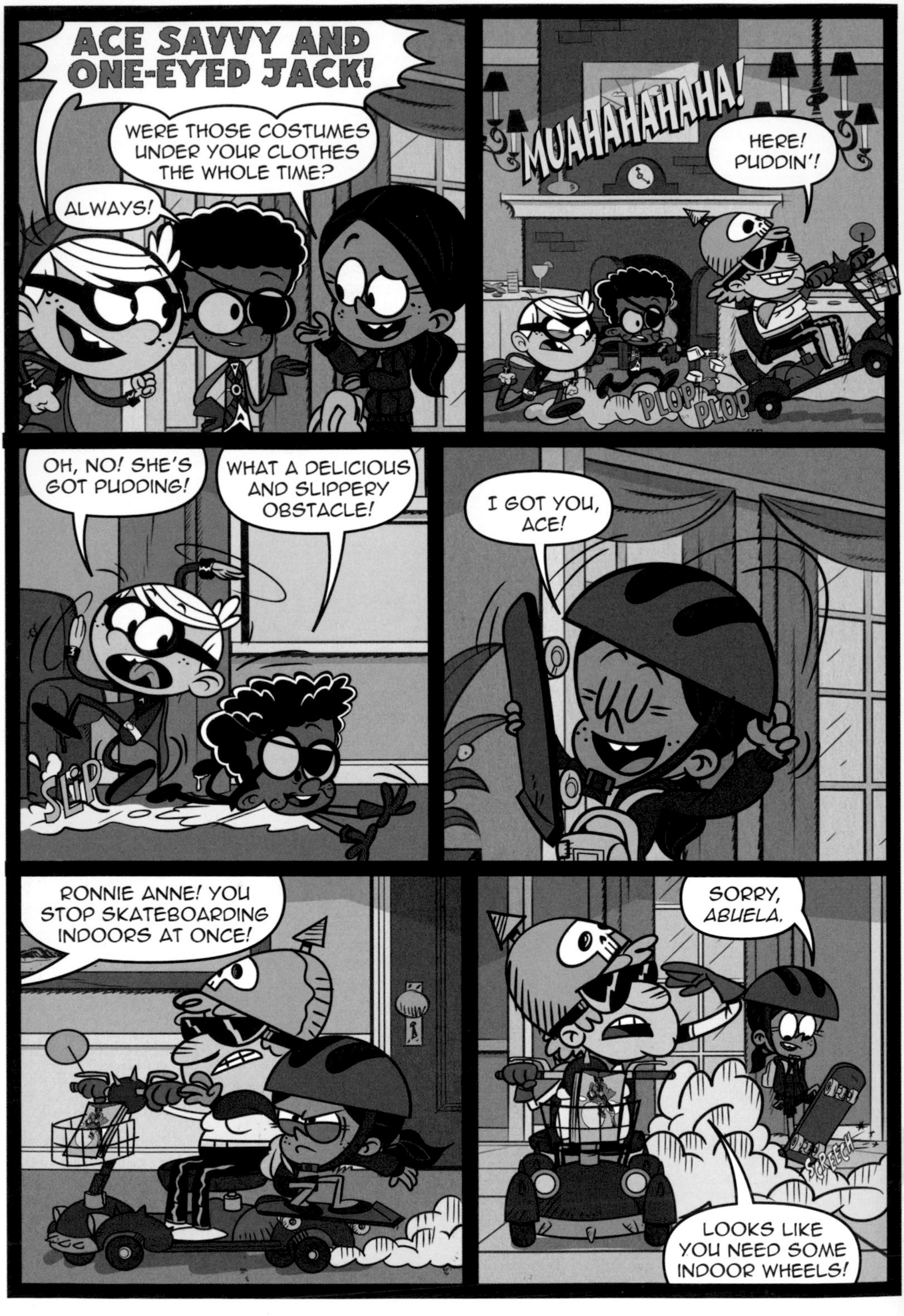
ACE SAVVY AND ONE-EYED JACK!
WERE THOSE COSTUMES UNDER YOUR CLOTHES THE WHOLE TIME?
ALWAYS!
MUAHAHAHAHA!
HERE! PUDDIN'!
PLOP PLOP
OH, NO! SHE'S GOT PUDDING!
WHAT A DELICIOUS AND SLIPPERY OBSTACLE!
SLIP
I GOT YOU, ACE!
RONNIE ANNE! YOU STOP SKATEBOARDING INDOORS AT ONCE!
SORRY, ABUELA.
SCREECH
LOOKS LIKE YOU NEED SOME INDOOR WHEELS!

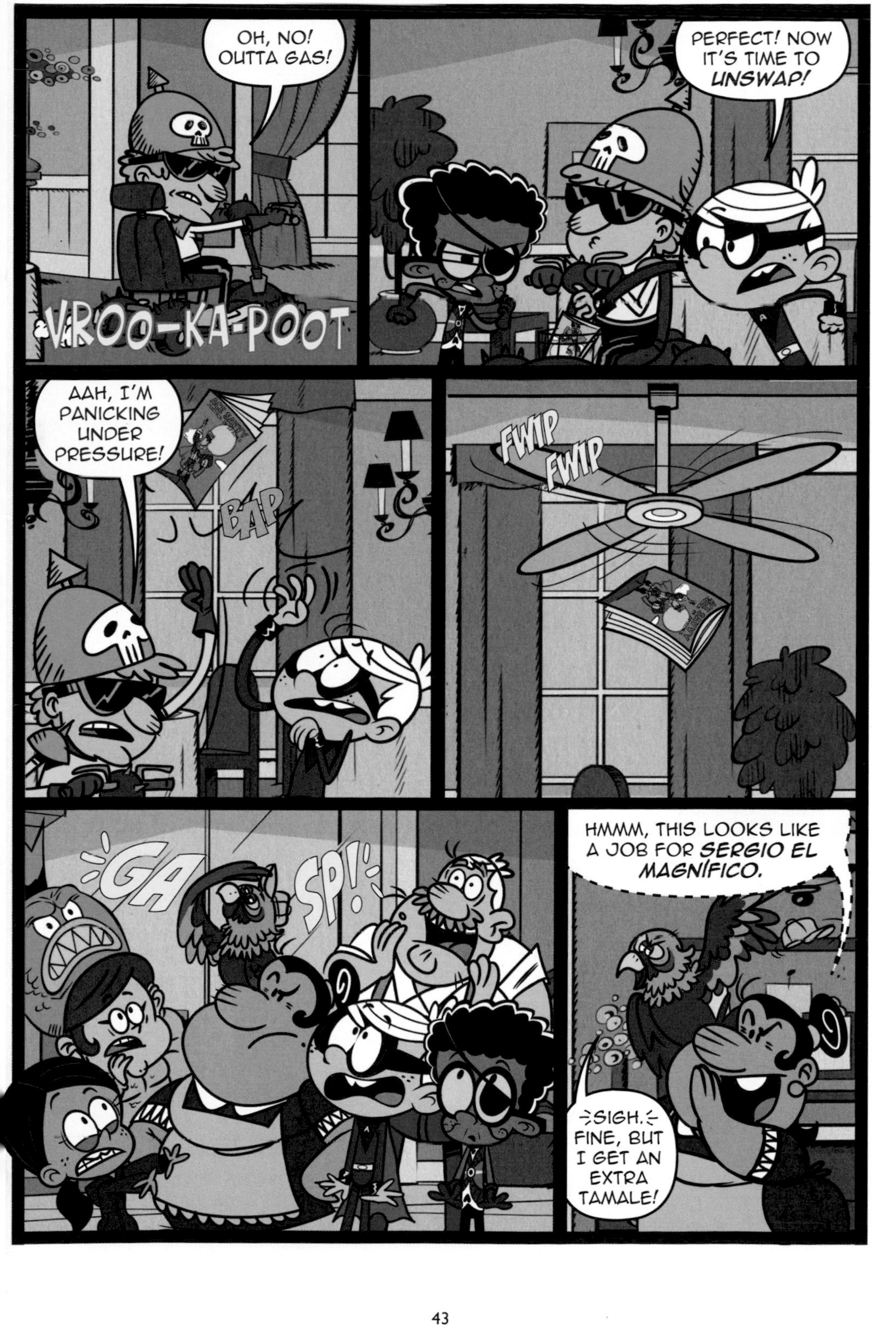
OH, NO! OUTTA GAS!
VROO-KA-POOT
PERFECT! NOW IT'S TIME TO UNSWAP!
AAH, I'M PANICKING UNDER PRESSURE!
BAP
FWIP FWIP
GASP!
HMMM, THIS LOOKS LIKE A JOB FOR SERGIO EL MAGNÍFICO.
SIGH. FINE, BUT I GET AN EXTRA TAMALE!

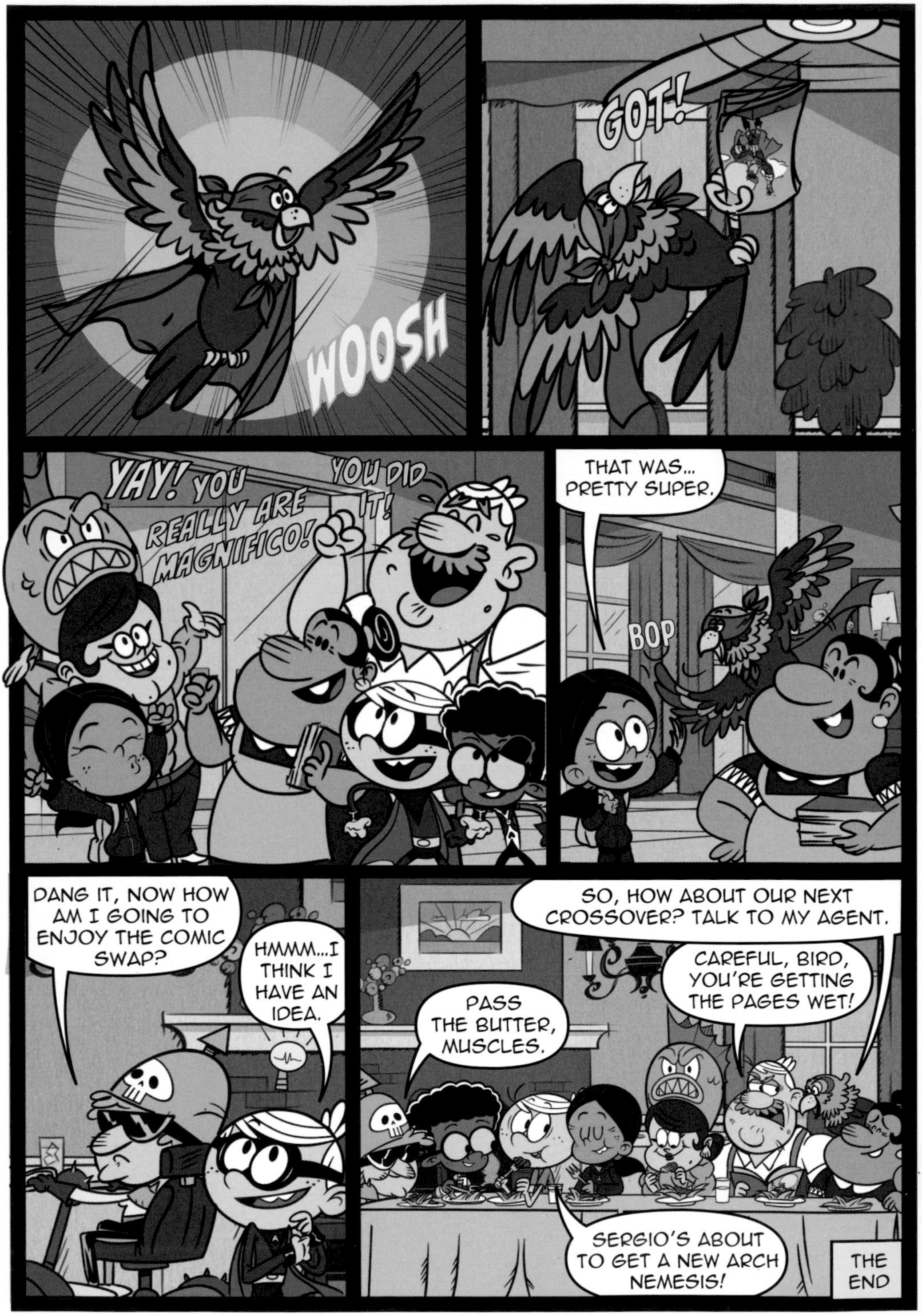
WOOSH
GOT!
YAY! YOU REALLY ARE MAGNIFICO!
YOU DID IT!
THAT WAS... PRETTY SUPER.
BOP
DANG IT, NOW HOW AM I GOING TO ENJOY THE COMIC SWAP?
HMMM...I THINK I HAVE AN IDEA.
SO, HOW ABOUT OUR NEXT CROSSOVER? TALK TO MY AGENT.
CAREFUL, BIRD, YOU'RE GETTING THE PAGES WET!
PASS THE BUTTER, MUSCLES.
SERGIO'S ABOUT TO GET A NEW ARCH NEMESIS!
THE END

"CASA CAMPERS"

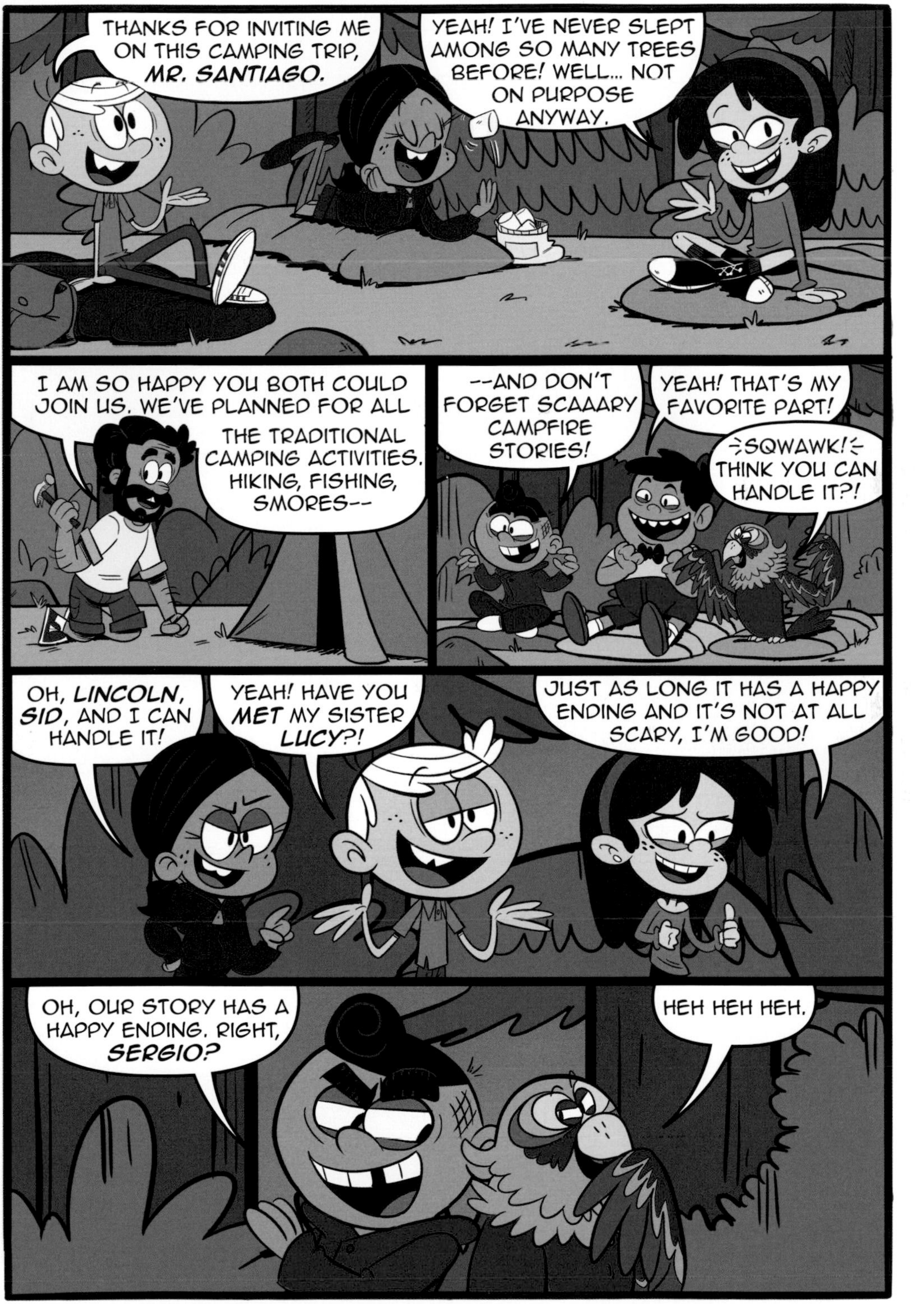
THANKS FOR INVITING ME ON THIS CAMPING TRIP, MR. SANTIAGO.
YEAH! I'VE NEVER SLEPT AMONG SO MANY TREES BEFORE! WELL... NOT ON PURPOSE ANYWAY.
I AM SO HAPPY YOU BOTH COULD JOIN US. WE'VE PLANNED FOR ALL THE TRADITIONAL CAMPING ACTIVITIES. HIKING, FISHING, SMORES--
--AND DON'T FORGET SCAAARY CAMPFIRE STORIES!
YEAH! THAT'S MY FAVORITE PART!
SQWAWK! THINK YOU CAN HANDLE IT?!
OH, LINCOLN, SID, AND I CAN HANDLE IT!
YEAH! HAVE YOU MET MY SISTER LUCY?!
JUST AS LONG IT HAS A HAPPY ENDING AND IT'S NOT AT ALL SCARY, I'M GOOD!
OH, OUR STORY HAS A HAPPY ENDING. RIGHT, SERGIO?
HEH HEH HEH.

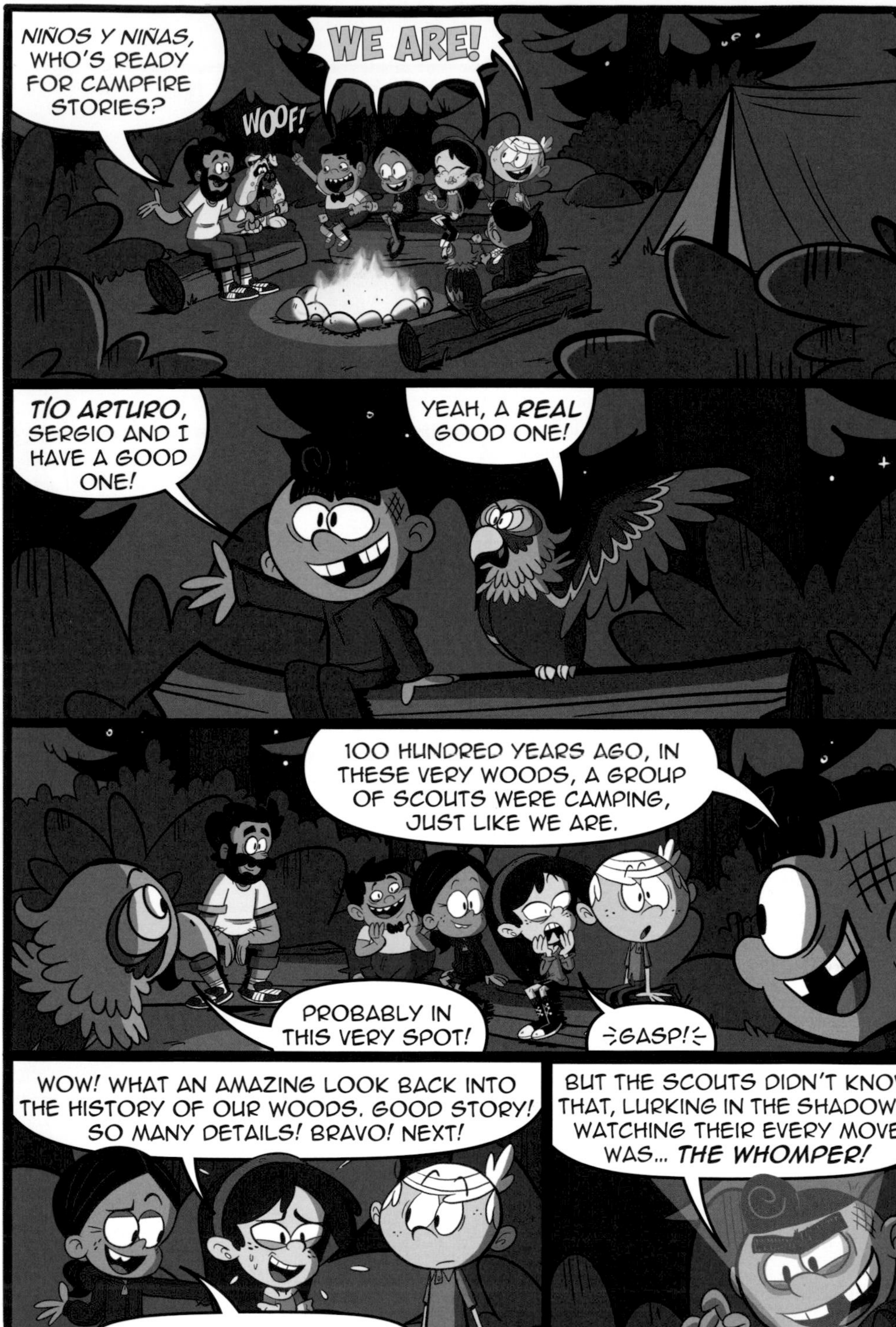
NIÑOS Y NIÑAS, WHO'S READY FOR CAMPFIRE STORIES?
WE ARE!
WOOF!
TÍO ARTURO, SERGIO AND I HAVE A GOOD ONE!
YEAH, A REAL GOOD ONE!
100 HUNDRED YEARS AGO, IN THESE VERY WOODS, A GROUP OF SCOUTS WERE CAMPING, JUST LIKE WE ARE.
PROBABLY IN THIS VERY SPOT!
GASP!
WOW! WHAT AN AMAZING LOOK BACK INTO THE HISTORY OF OUR WOODS. GOOD STORY! SO MANY DETAILS! BRAVO! NEXT!
COME ON, SID, IT'S JUST A STORY. LET'S KEEP GOING!
BUT THE SCOUTS DIDN'T KNOW THAT, LURKING IN THE SHADOWS, WATCHING THEIR EVERY MOVE WAS... THE WHOMPER!

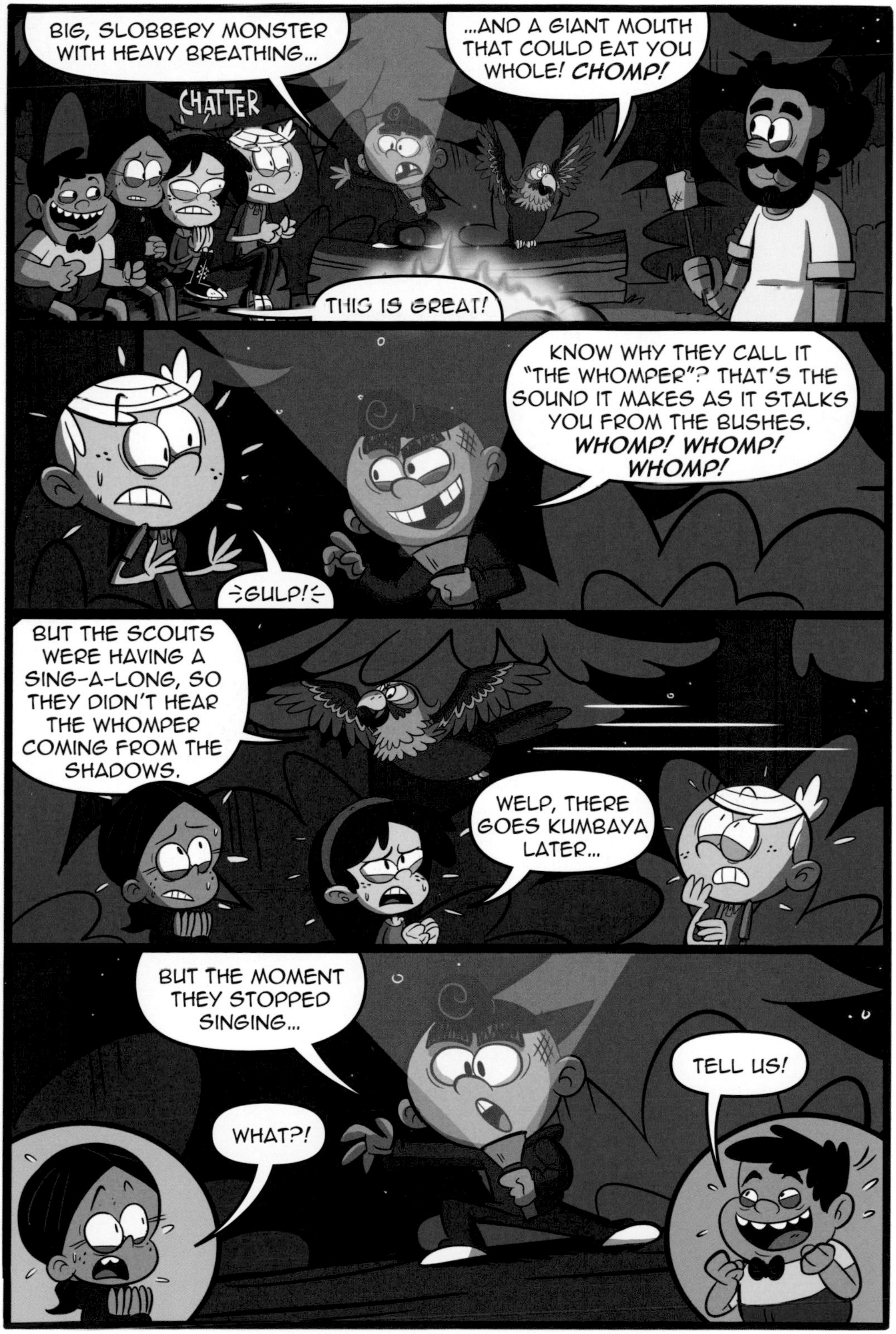
BIG, SLOBBERY MONSTER WITH HEAVY BREATHING...
CHATTER
...AND A GIANT MOUTH THAT COULD EAT YOU WHOLE! CHOMP!
THIS IS GREAT!
KNOW WHY THEY CALL IT "THE WHOMPER"? THAT'S THE SOUND IT MAKES AS IT STALKS YOU FROM THE BUSHES. WHOMP! WHOMP! WHOMP!
GULP!
BUT THE SCOUTS WERE HAVING A SING-A-LONG, SO THEY DIDN'T HEAR THE WHOMPER COMING FROM THE SHADOWS.
WELP, THERE GOES KUMBAYA LATER...
BUT THE MOMENT THEY STOPPED SINGING...
TELL US!
WHAT?!

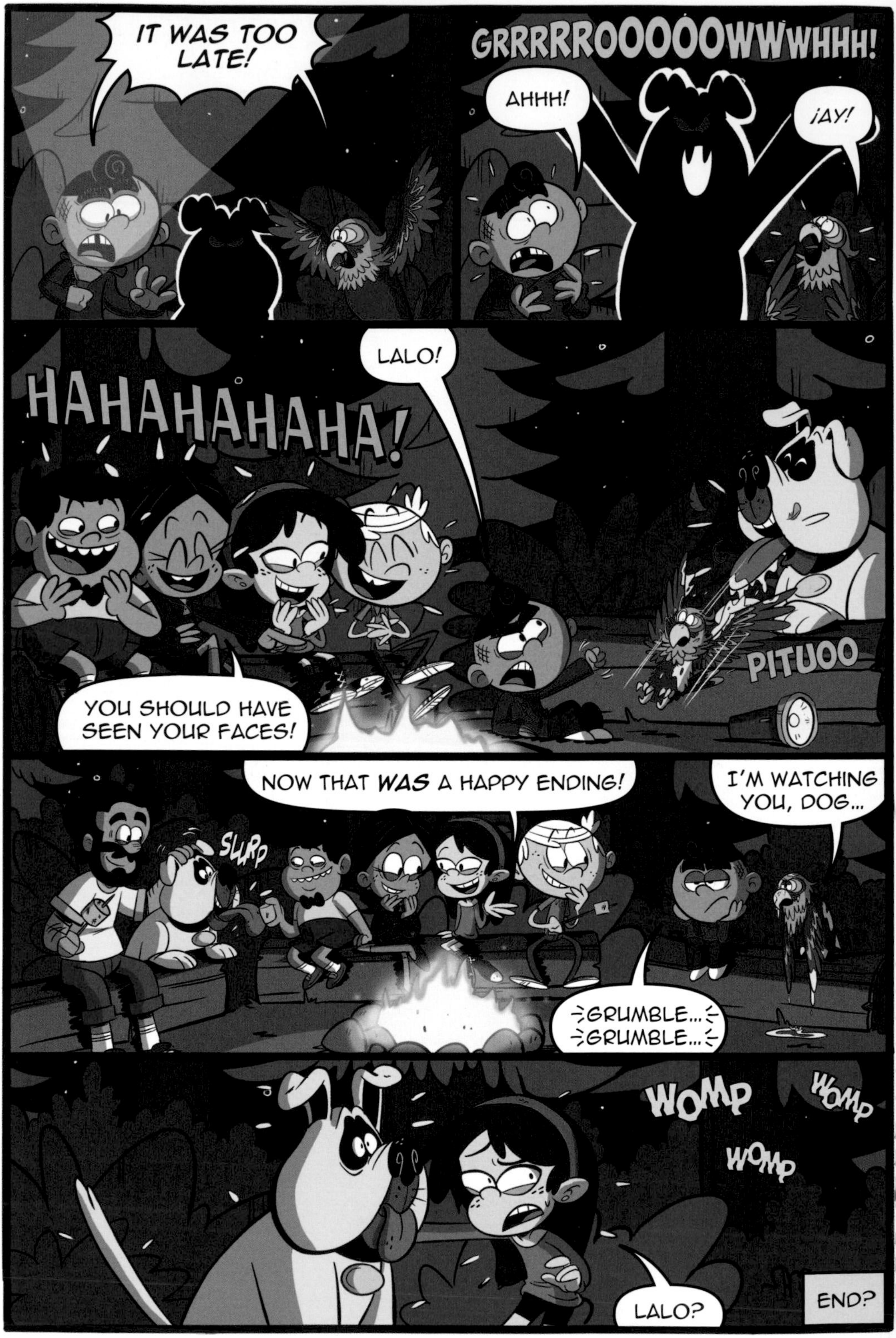
IT WAS TOO LATE!
GRRRRROOOOOWWWHHH!
AHHH!
¡AY!
HAHAHAHAHA!
LALO!
YOU SHOULD HAVE SEEN YOUR FACES!
PITUOO
NOW THAT WAS A HAPPY ENDING!
SLURP
I'M WATCHING YOU, DOG...
GRUMBLE... GRUMBLE...
WOMP
WOMP
WOMP
LALO?
END?

"¡Tu Destino!"

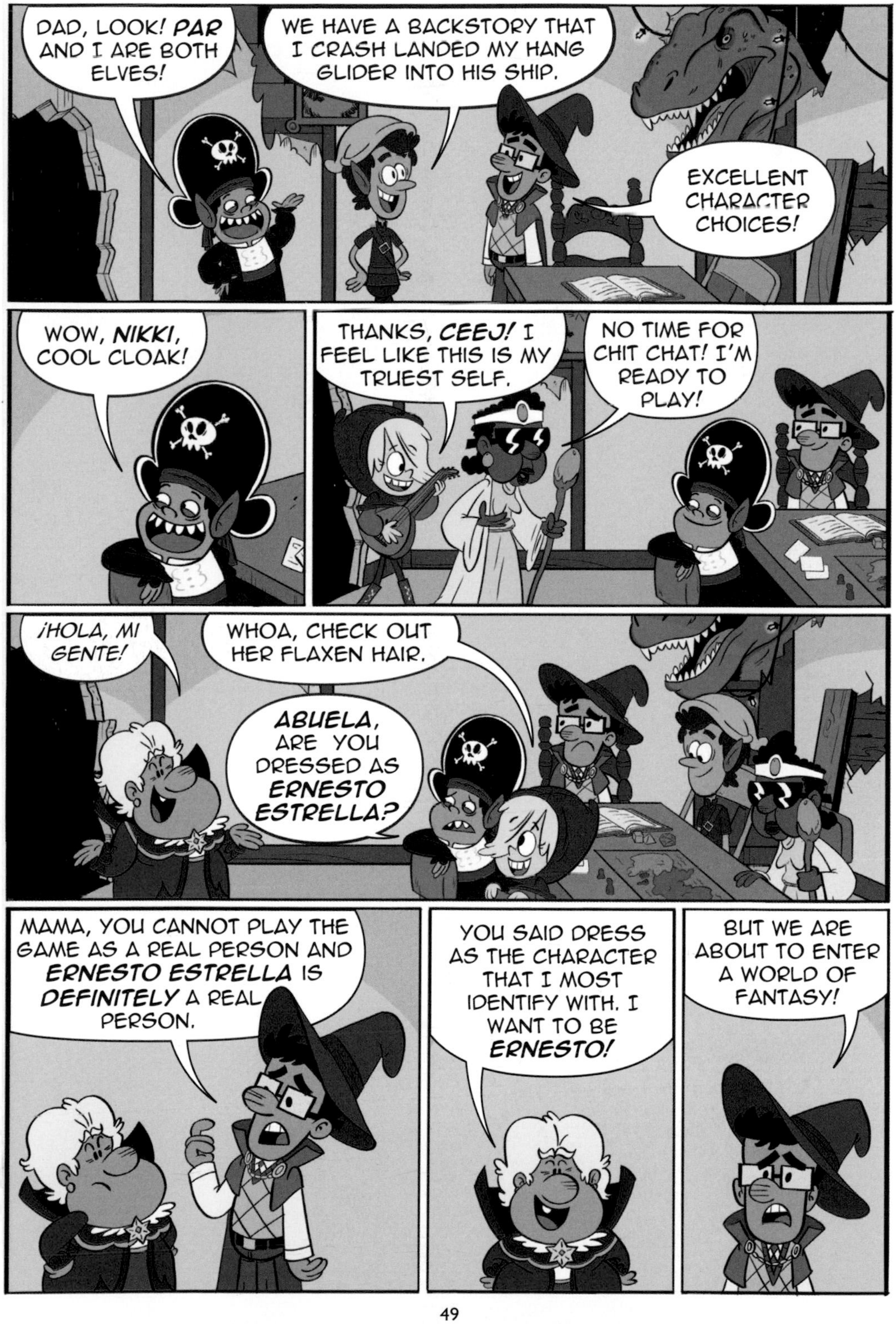
DAD, LOOK! PAR AND I ARE BOTH ELVES!
WE HAVE A BACKSTORY THAT I CRASH LANDED MY HANG GLIDER INTO HIS SHIP.
EXCELLENT CHARACTER CHOICES!
WOW, NIKKI, COOL CLOAK!
THANKS, CEEJ! I FEEL LIKE THIS IS MY TRUEST SELF.
NO TIME FOR CHIT CHAT! I'M READY TO PLAY!
¡HOLA, MI GENTE!
WHOA, CHECK OUT HER FLAXEN HAIR.
ABUELA, ARE YOU DRESSED AS ERNESTO ESTRELLA?
MAMA, YOU CANNOT PLAY THE GAME AS A REAL PERSON AND ERNESTO ESTRELLA IS DEFINITELY A REAL PERSON.
YOU SAID DRESS AS THE CHARACTER THAT I MOST IDENTIFY WITH. I WANT TO BE ERNESTO!
BUT WE ARE ABOUT TO ENTER A WORLD OF FANTASY!

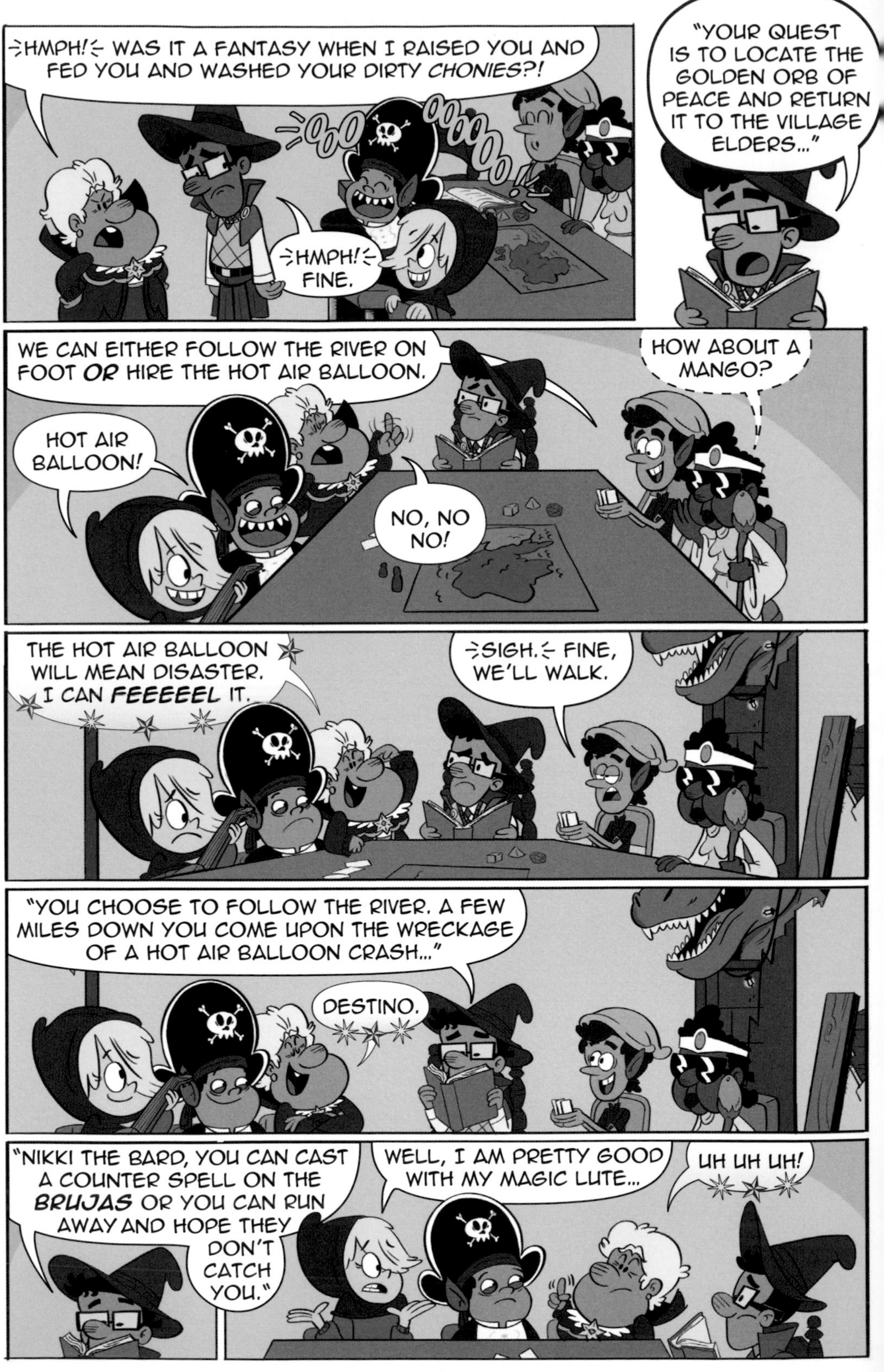
HMPH! WAS IT A FANTASY WHEN I RAISED YOU AND FED YOU AND WASHED YOUR DIRTY *CHONIES*?!
OOOOOOOOO
HMPH! FINE.
"YOUR QUEST IS TO LOCATE THE GOLDEN ORB OF PEACE AND RETURN IT TO THE VILLAGE ELDERS..."
WE CAN EITHER FOLLOW THE RIVER ON FOOT ***OR*** HIRE THE HOT AIR BALLOON.
HOW ABOUT A MANGO?
HOT AIR BALLOON!
NO, NO NO!
THE HOT AIR BALLOON WILL MEAN DISASTER. I CAN ***FEEEEEL*** IT.
SIGH. FINE, WE'LL WALK.
"YOU CHOOSE TO FOLLOW THE RIVER. A FEW MILES DOWN YOU COME UPON THE WRECKAGE OF A HOT AIR BALLOON CRASH..."
DESTINO.
"NIKKI THE BARD, YOU CAN CAST A COUNTER SPELL ON THE ***BRUJAS*** OR YOU CAN RUN AWAY AND HOPE THEY DON'T CATCH YOU."
WELL, I AM PRETTY GOOD WITH MY MAGIC LUTE...
UH UH UH!

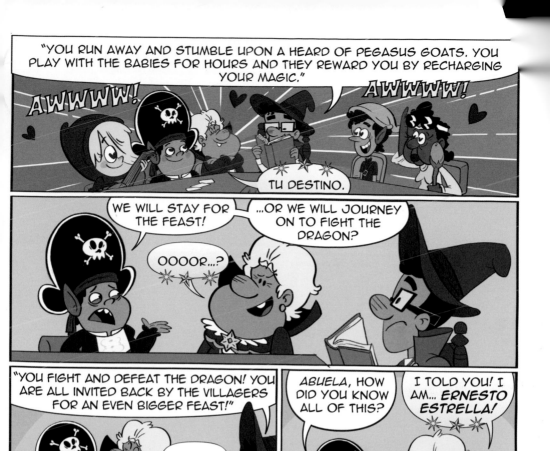

"YOU RUN AWAY AND STUMBLE UPON A HEARD OF PEGASUS GOATS. YOU PLAY WITH THE BABIES FOR HOURS AND THEY REWARD YOU BY RECHARGING YOUR MAGIC."

AWWWW!

AWWWW!

TU DESTINO.

WE WILL STAY FOR THE FEAST!

...OR WE WILL JOURNEY ON TO FIGHT THE DRAGON?

OOOOR...?

"YOU FIGHT AND DEFEAT THE DRAGON! YOU ARE ALL INVITED BACK BY THE VILLAGERS FOR AN EVEN BIGGER FEAST!"

YAAAAAY!

ABUELA, HOW DID YOU KNOW ALL OF THIS?

I TOLD YOU! I AM... *ERNESTO ESTRELLA!*

THAT HAS TO BE AGAINST THE RULES.

YOU WANT TO TELL HER? ⸮GULP!⸮

CHOMP

END

"WASHED UP"

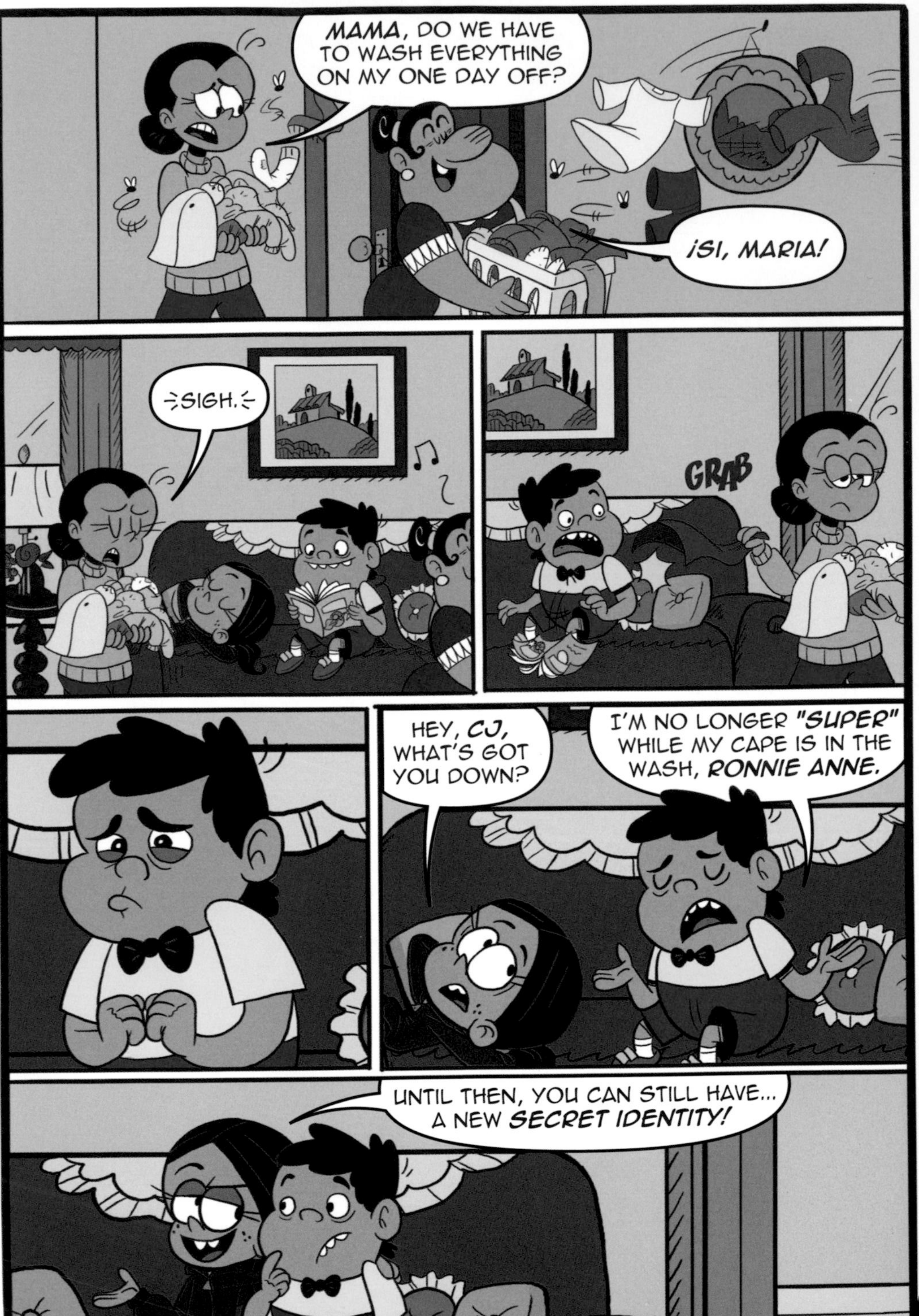
MAMA, DO WE HAVE TO WASH EVERYTHING ON MY ONE DAY OFF?
¡SI, MARIA!
SIGH.
GRAB
HEY, CJ, WHAT'S GOT YOU DOWN?
I'M NO LONGER "SUPER" WHILE MY CAPE IS IN THE WASH, RONNIE ANNE.
UNTIL THEN, YOU CAN STILL HAVE... A NEW SECRET IDENTITY!

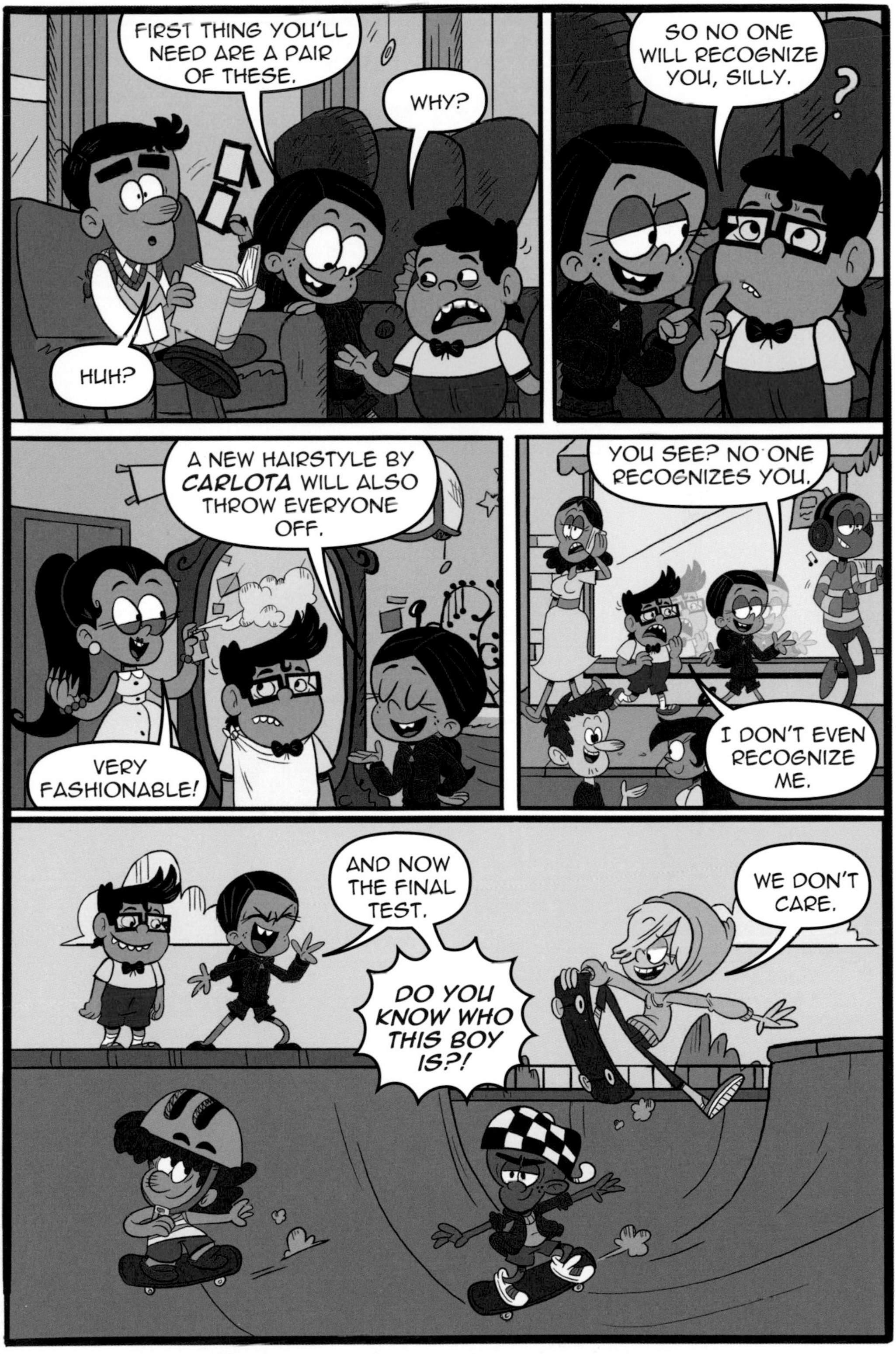
FIRST THING YOU'LL NEED ARE A PAIR OF THESE.
HUH?
WHY?
SO NO ONE WILL RECOGNIZE YOU, SILLY.
?
A NEW HAIRSTYLE BY CARLOTA WILL ALSO THROW EVERYONE OFF.
VERY FASHIONABLE!
YOU SEE? NO ONE RECOGNIZES YOU.
I DON'T EVEN RECOGNIZE ME.
AND NOW THE FINAL TEST.
DO YOU KNOW WHO THIS BOY IS?!
WE DON'T CARE.

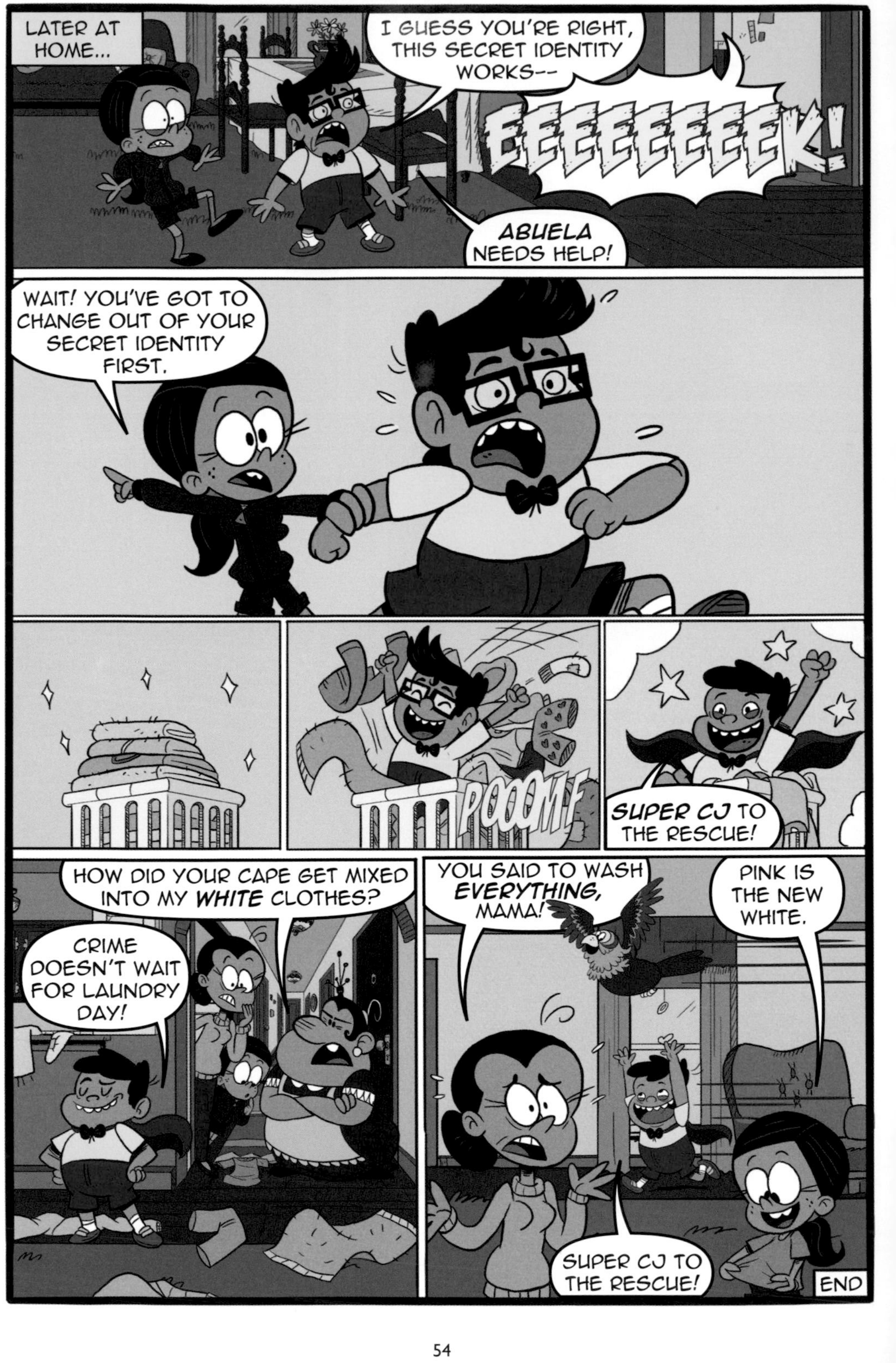
LATER AT HOME...
I GUESS YOU'RE RIGHT, THIS SECRET IDENTITY WORKS--
EEEEEEEEEK!
ABUELA NEEDS HELP!
WAIT! YOU'VE GOT TO CHANGE OUT OF YOUR SECRET IDENTITY FIRST.
POOOMF
SUPER CJ TO THE RESCUE!
HOW DID YOUR CAPE GET MIXED INTO MY WHITE CLOTHES?
CRIME DOESN'T WAIT FOR LAUNDRY DAY!
YOU SAID TO WASH EVERYTHING, MAMA!
PINK IS THE NEW WHITE.
SUPER CJ TO THE RESCUE!
END

"UNBREAK-A-BULL"

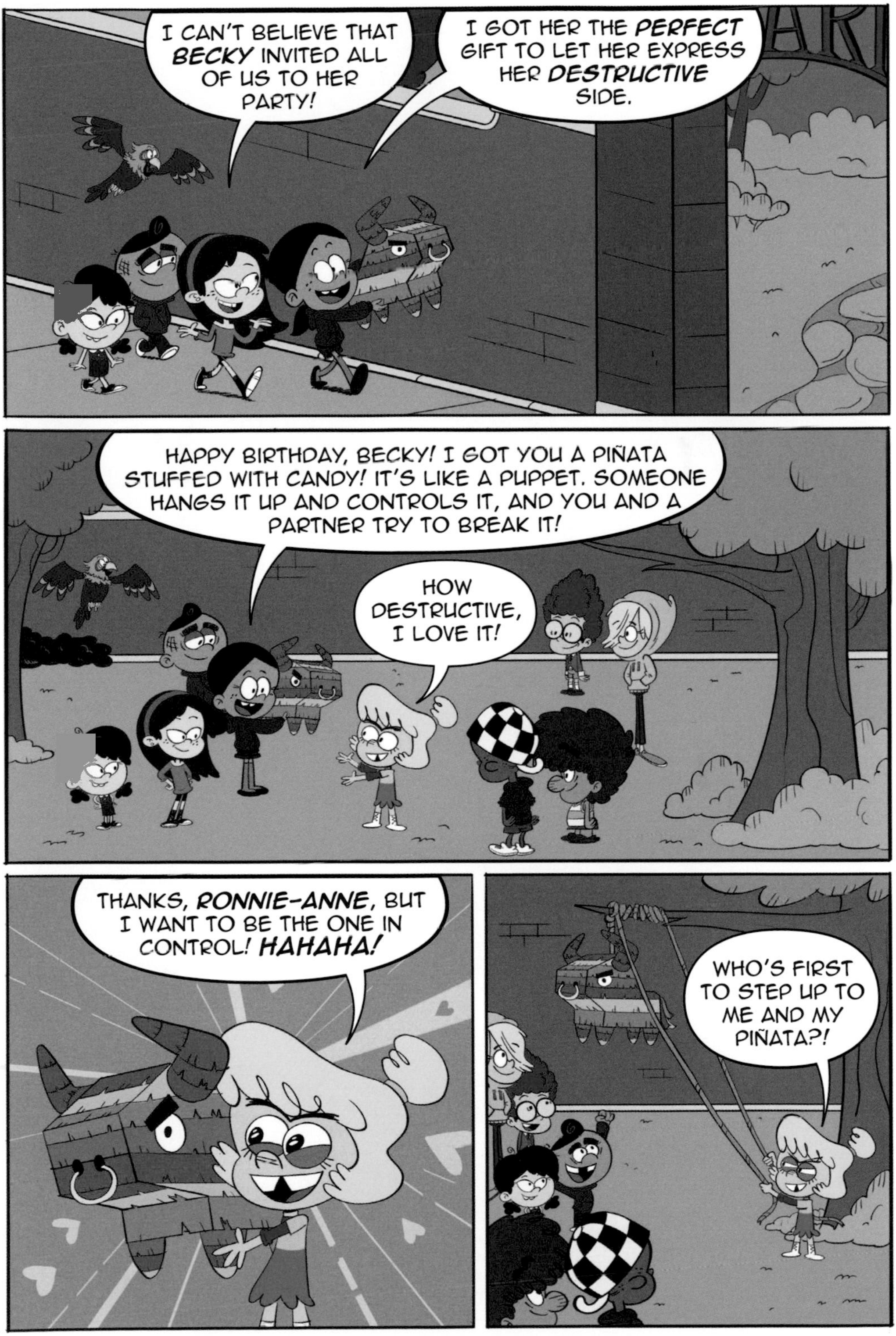
I CAN'T BELIEVE THAT BECKY INVITED ALL OF US TO HER PARTY!
I GOT HER THE PERFECT GIFT TO LET HER EXPRESS HER DESTRUCTIVE SIDE.
HAPPY BIRTHDAY, BECKY! I GOT YOU A PIÑATA STUFFED WITH CANDY! IT'S LIKE A PUPPET. SOMEONE HANGS IT UP AND CONTROLS IT, AND YOU AND A PARTNER TRY TO BREAK IT!
HOW DESTRUCTIVE, I LOVE IT!
THANKS, RONNIE-ANNE, BUT I WANT TO BE THE ONE IN CONTROL! HAHAHA!
WHO'S FIRST TO STEP UP TO ME AND MY PIÑATA?!

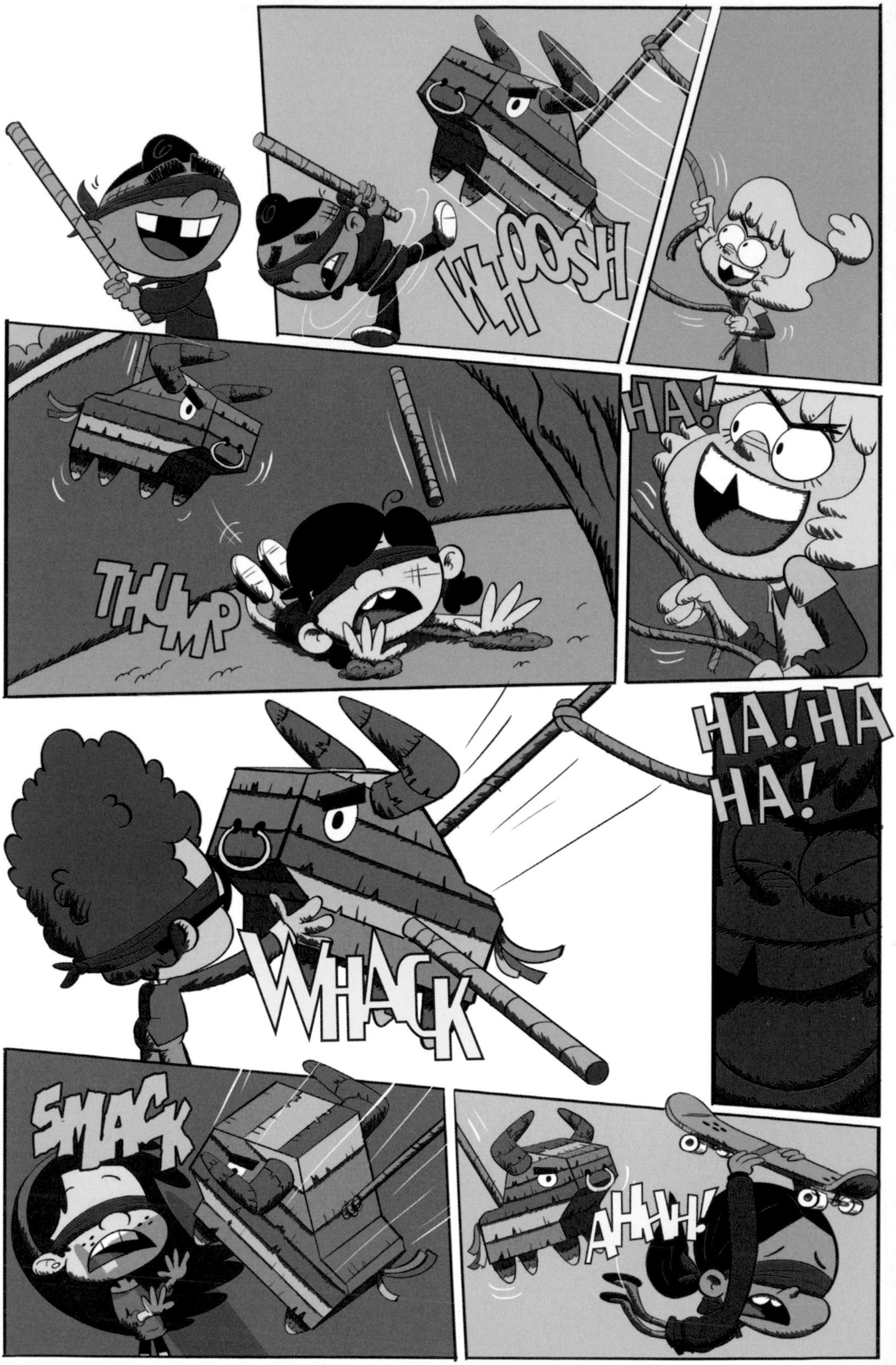
WHOOSH
THUMP
HA!
HA! HA HA!
WHACK
SMACK
AHHH!

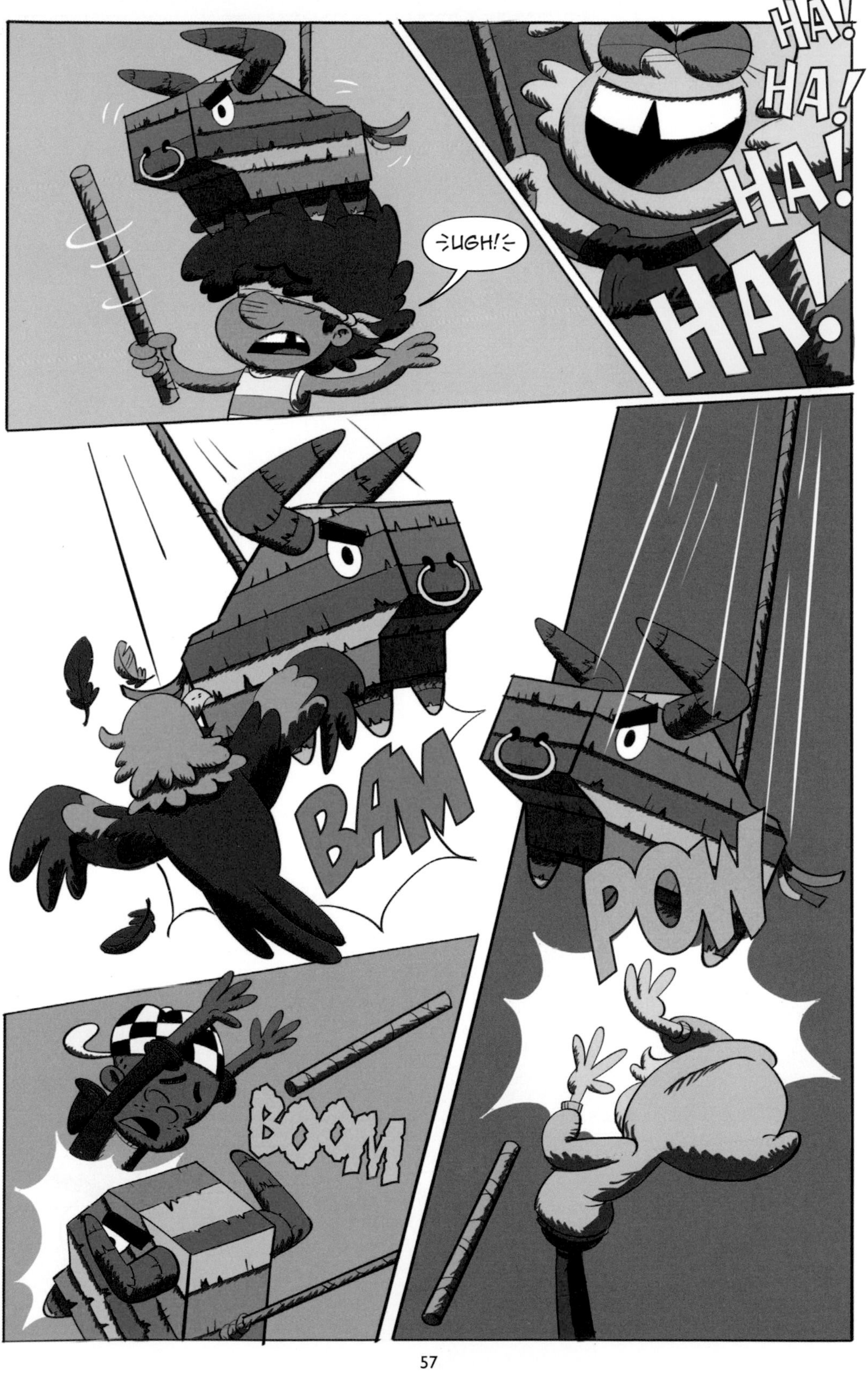
UGH!
HA! HA! HA! HA!
BAM
POW
BOOM

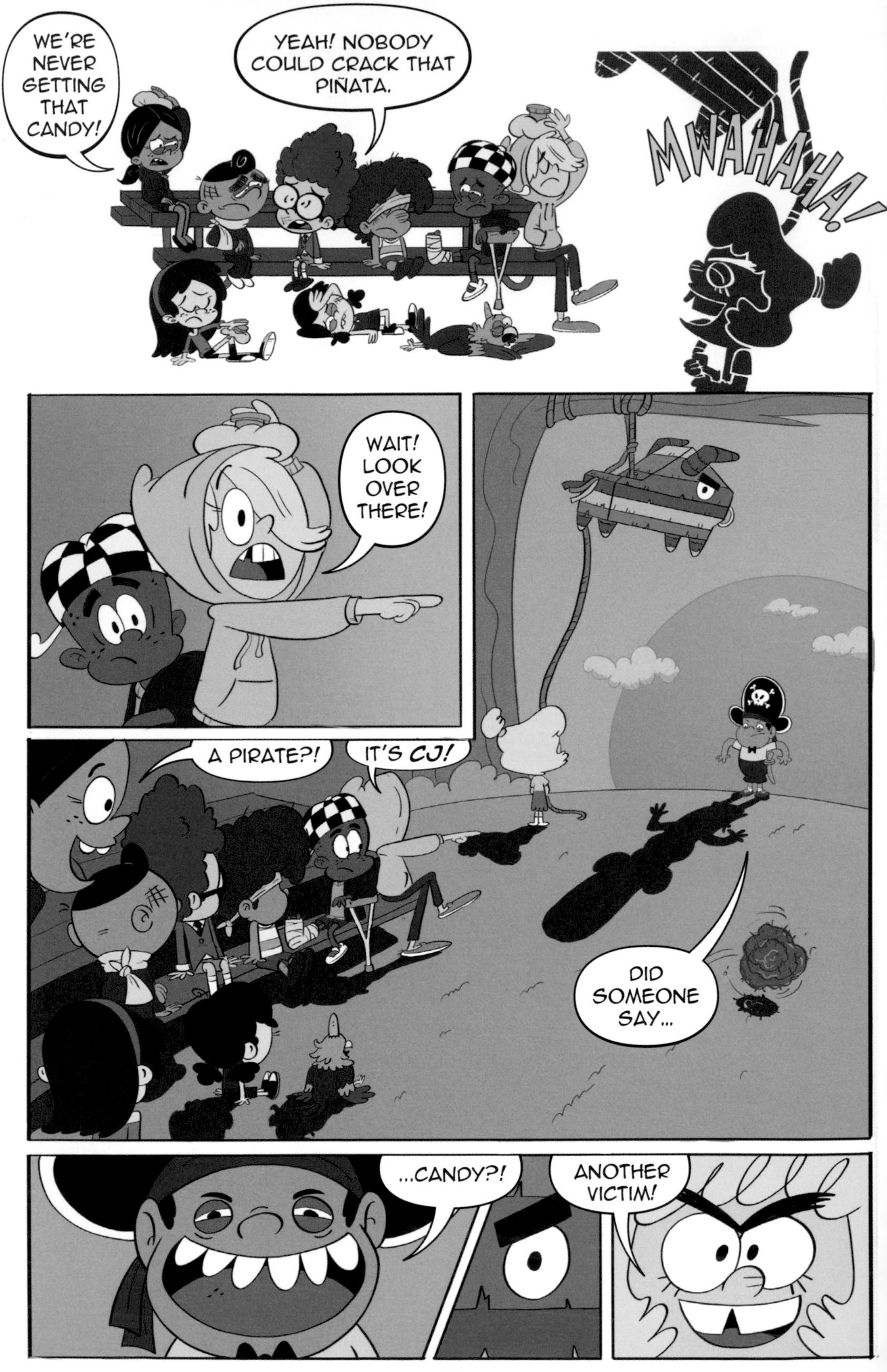
WE'RE NEVER GETTING THAT CANDY!
YEAH! NOBODY COULD CRACK THAT PIÑATA.
MWAHAHAHA!
WAIT! LOOK OVER THERE!
A PIRATE?!
IT'S CJ!
DID SOMEONE SAY...
...CANDY?!
ANOTHER VICTIM!

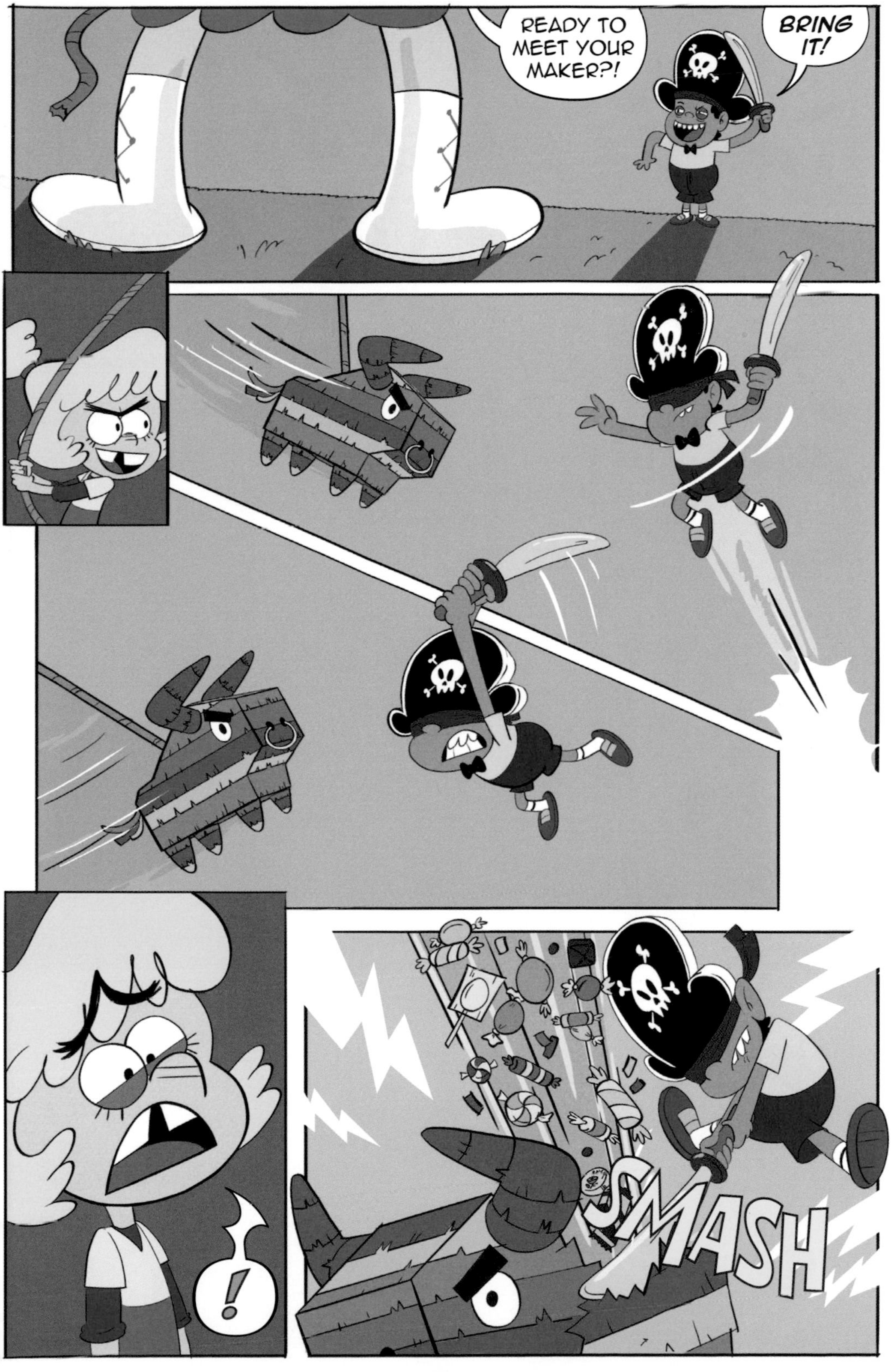
READY TO MEET YOUR MAKER?!
BRING IT!
!
SMASH

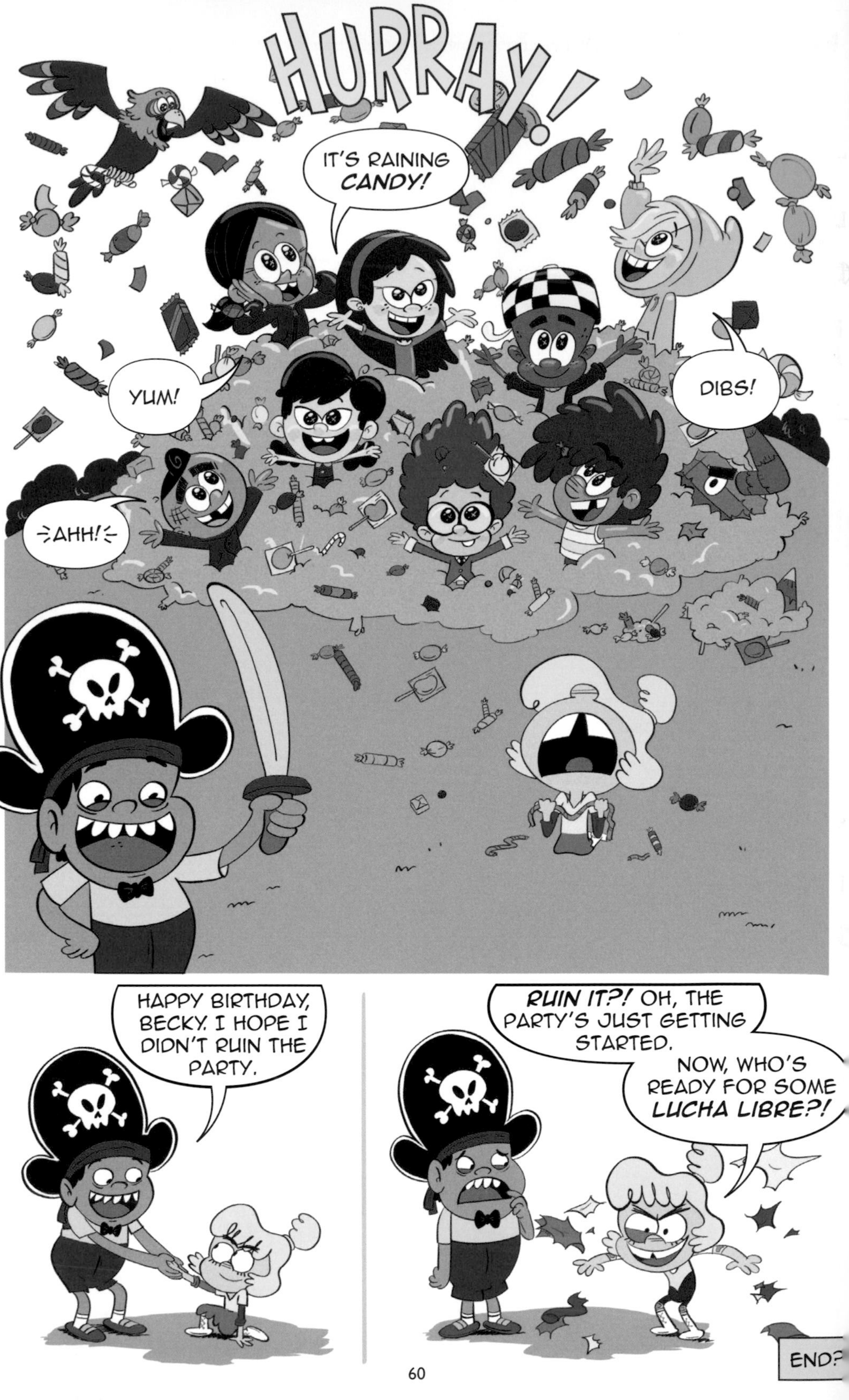
HURRAY!
IT'S RAINING CANDY!
YUM!
DIBS!
AHH!
HAPPY BIRTHDAY, BECKY. I HOPE I DIDN'T RUIN THE PARTY.
RUIN IT?! OH, THE PARTY'S JUST GETTING STARTED.
NOW, WHO'S READY FOR SOME LUCHA LIBRE?!
END?

BONUS: BEHIND-THE-SCENES, EXPLORING THE CASAGRANDES' APARTMENT BUILDING

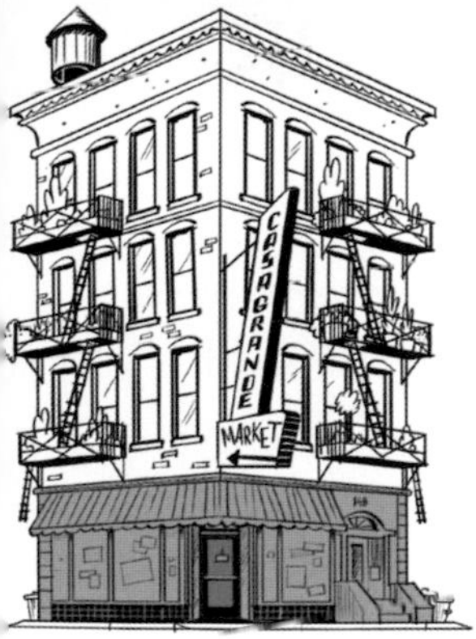
CASAGRANDE
MARKET

1ST FLOOR

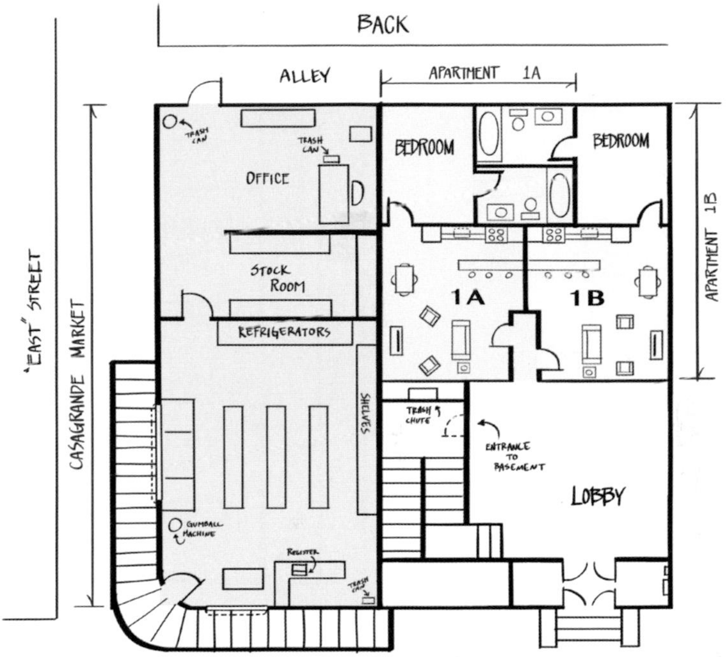
BACK
ALLEY
APARTMENT 1A
BEDROOM
BEDROOM
APARTMENT 1B
TRASH CAN
TRASH CAN
OFFICE
STOCK ROOM
REFRIGERATORS
SHELVES
1A
1B
"EAST" STREET
CASAGRANDE MARKET
TRASH & CHUTE
ENTRANCE TO BASEMENT
LOBBY
GUMBALL MACHINE
REGISTER
TRASH CAN

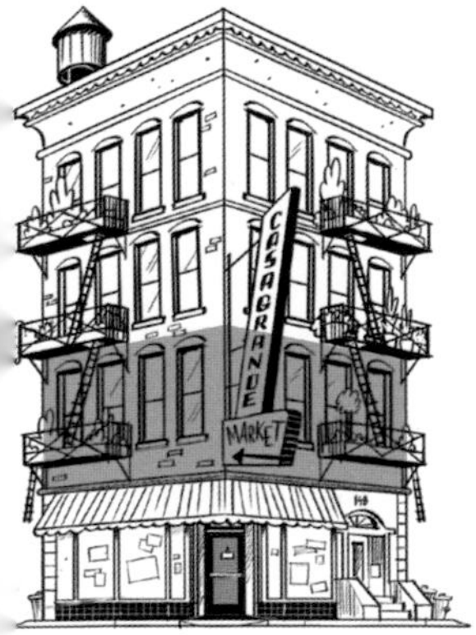
CASAGRANDE
MARKET

2ND FLOOR

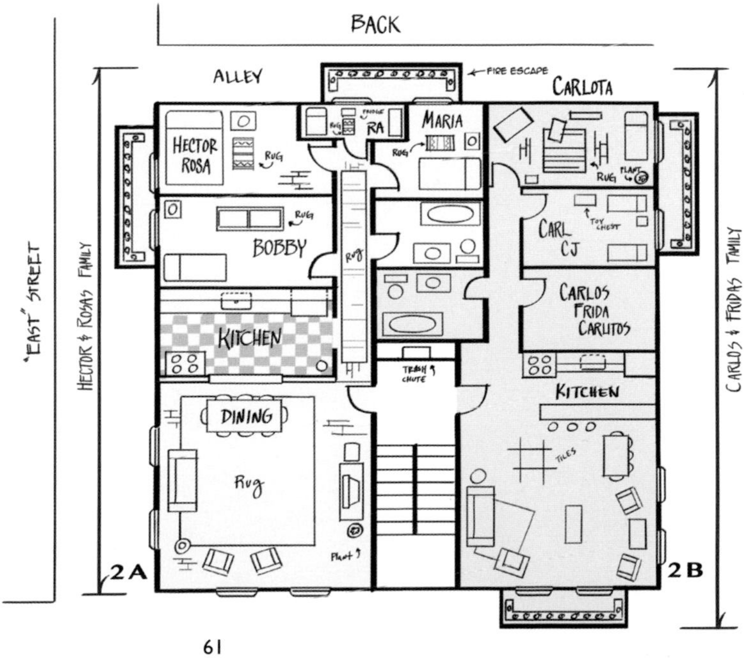
BACK
ALLEY
FIRE ESCAPE
CARLOTA
HECTOR ROSA
RUG
FRIDGE
RA
MARIA
RUG
RUG
PLANT
BOBBY
RUG
Rug
CARL CJ
TOY CHEST
CARLOS FRIDA CARLITOS
KITCHEN
TRASH & CHUTE
KITCHEN
DINING
Rug
TILES
Plant
2A
2B
"EAST" STREET
HECTOR & ROSA'S FAMILY
CARLOS & FRIDA'S FAMILY

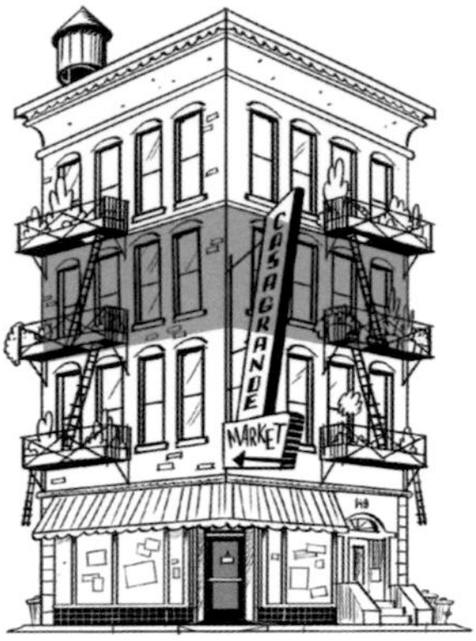
CASAGRANDE
MARKET

3RD FLOOR

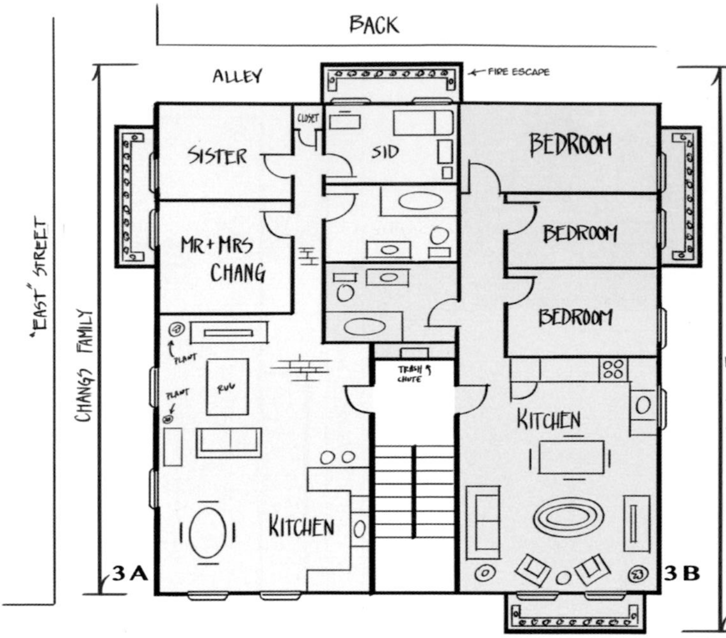
BACK
ALLEY
FIRE ESCAPE
CLOSET
SISTER
SID
BEDROOM
BEDROOM
MR + MRS CHANG
BEDROOM
PLANT
PLANT
RUG
TRASH CHUTE
KITCHEN
KITCHEN
3A
3B
"EAST" STREET
CHANGS FAMILY
FLORES FAMILY

BONUS: BEHIND-THE-SCENES, EXPLORING THE CASAGRANDES' NEIGHBORHOOD

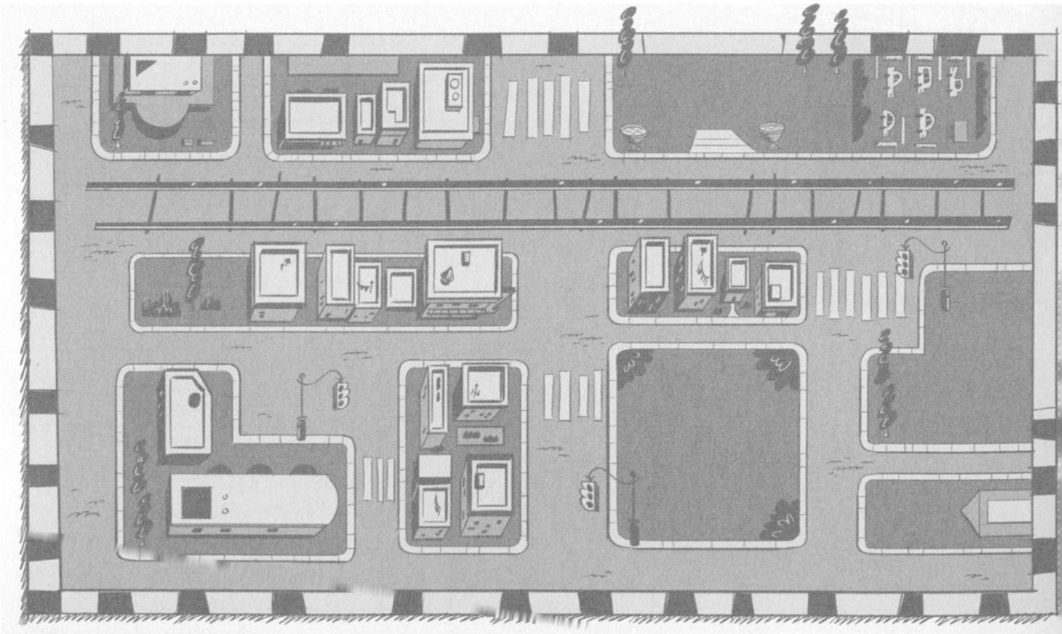

WATCH OUT FOR PAPERCUTZ

¡Hola! Welcome to the fun(and food)-filled THE CASAGRANDES #2 "Anything for Familia," from Papercutz, those fun(and food)-loving folks dedicated to publishing great graphic novels for all ages. I'm Jim Salicrup, the Editor-in-Chief and Lalo's part-time walker, here to tell you about some of the other Papercutz graphic novels we suspect you might enjoy…

nickelodeon
3 GRAPHIC NOVELS IN 1
INCLUDES "THERE WILL BE CHAOS" "THERE WILL BE MORE CHAOS" "LIVE LIFE LOUD!"
THE LOUD HOUSE
PAPERCUTZ

3 (•••) SMURFS GRAPHIC NOVELS IN 1 BY Peyo
THE SMURFS
3 IN 1
THE ASTROSMURF
THE SMURF APPRENTICE
GARGAMEL AND THE SMURFS
PAPERCUTZ

First there's THE LOUD HOUSE… Now, some of you might be saying, "Come on, Jim, we all know about THE LOUD HOUSE graphic novels that Papercutz has been publishing! After all, most of the stories in this graphic novel come from the pages of THE LOUD HOUSE graphic novels." Well, the fact that all the stories collected here are from THE LOUD HOUSE is true—except for "Let's Ketchup," "Mission ImPAWSible," and "Un-Break-a-Bull," which are all-new— but believe it or not, there are some folks who haven't yet seen THE LOUD HOUSE. That CASAGRANDES is their first experience in this particular cartoon universe. (Side note: THE CASAGRANDES #3 will be totally full of all-new stories!) So, letting them know that Lincoln, the crazy white-haired boy who is Ronnie Anne's friend also appears (along with his ten sisters, Lori, Leni, Luna, Luan, Lynn, Lucy, Lola, Lana, Lisa, and Lily) not only on Nickelodeon's hit animated series THE LOUD HOUSE, but in THE LOUD HOUSE graphic novels from Papercutz, is virtually a public service! After all, we don't want anyone missing out on all the fun that family gets itself into. Perhaps the best way to catch up on THE LOUD HOUSE graphic novels is to pick up THE LOUD HOUSE 3 IN 1 graphic novels—each book collects 3 entire graphic novels of THE LOUD HOUSE.

Another graphic novel series that features the stars of yet another hit Nickelodeon show is THE SMURFS TALES. But unlike THE LOUD HOUSE and THE CASAGRANDES, which both started out as animated shows and were then adapted into comics (often by the very same writers, animators, of the TV shows), The Smurfs started out originally in comics (created by Peyo) and then made the leap into animation. Papercutz has been publishing those comics for years, and we just launched THE SMURFS TALES to tie-in with the Smurfs' all-new animated Nickelodeon series. And don't worry about missing out on any of our previously published SMURFS books, just like THE LOUD HOUSE 3 IN 1 graphic novels, we're also publishing THE SMURFS 3 IN 1 graphic novels. So, if you enjoy the timeless adventures of Papa Smurf, Smurfette, Brainy Smurf, Hefty Smurf, and all the rest, we're sure you'll enjoy the original comics in which they first appeared. Dare I say that they're truly Smurftastic?!

In case you think I'm trying to sell you something, may I point out that most Papercutz graphic novels are available at your local public or school library. All you need is a valid Library Card and you can borrow these graphic novels for free. The only catch is that you have to bring them back.

We'd like to take this opportunity to thank our friend Nickelodeon comics editor, Joan Hilty, for all her invaluable help on the many Nickelodeon graphic novels we produced together (Remember NICKELODEON PANDEMONIUM?), and to wish her great success in her future endeavors. Not only is Joan a terrific editor, but she's a great writer and cartoonist as well, and we hope we get to see more of her comics soon.

And just in case you weren't paying close attention earlier, the next volume of THE CASAGRANDES, coming soon, will feature totally all-new stories, so be sure not to miss it!

Gracias,

Jim

STAY IN TOUCH!

EMAIL:	salicrup@papercutz.com
WEB:	papercutz.com
TWITTER:	@papercutzgn
INSTAGRAM:	@papercutzgn
FACEBOOK:	PAPERCUTZGRAPHICNOVELS
FANMAIL:	Papercutz, 160 Broadway, Suite 700, East Wing, New York, NY 10038

Go to papercutz.com and sign up for the free Papercutz e-newsletter!

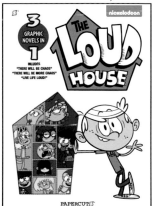

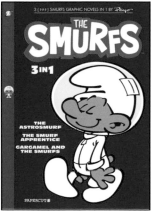

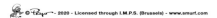

MORE GREAT GRAPHIC NOVEL SERIES AVAILABLE FROM PAPERCUTZ™

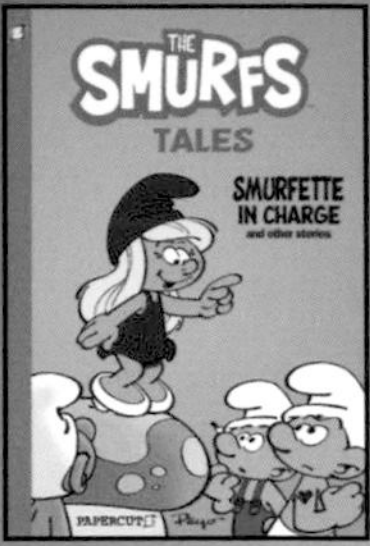
THE SMURFS
TALES
SMURFETTE IN CHARGE
and other stories
PAPERCUTZ
SMURFS TALES

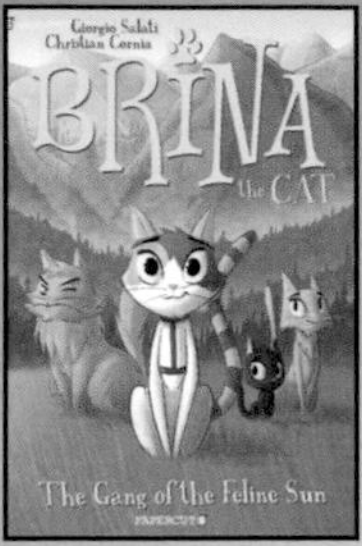
Giorgio Salati
Christian Cornia
BRINA
the CAT
The Gang of the Feline Sun
PAPERCUTZ
BRINA THE CAT

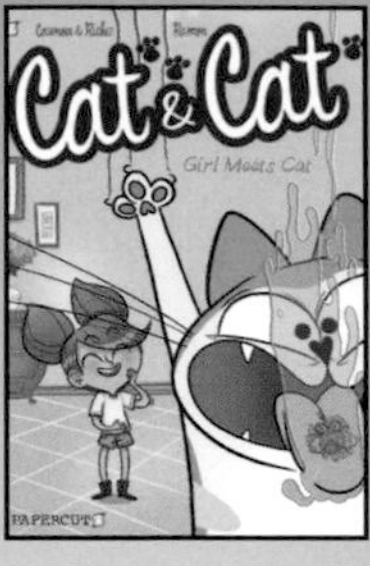
Cat & Cat
Girl Meets Cat
PAPERCUTZ
CAT & CAT

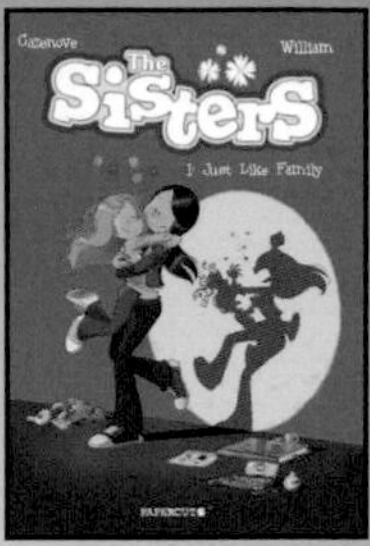
Cazenove
William
The Sisters
Just Like Family
PAPERCUTZ
THE SISTERS

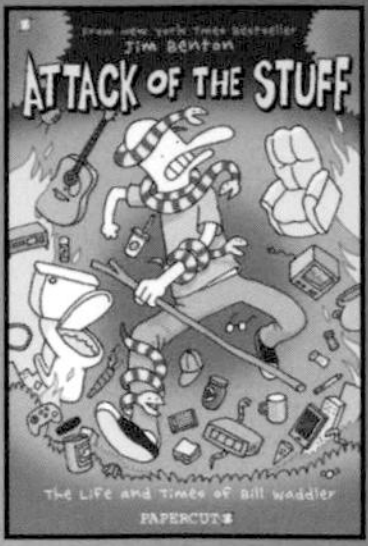
Jim Benton
ATTACK OF THE STUFF
The Life and Times of Bill Waddler
PAPERCUTZ
ATTACK OF THE STUFF

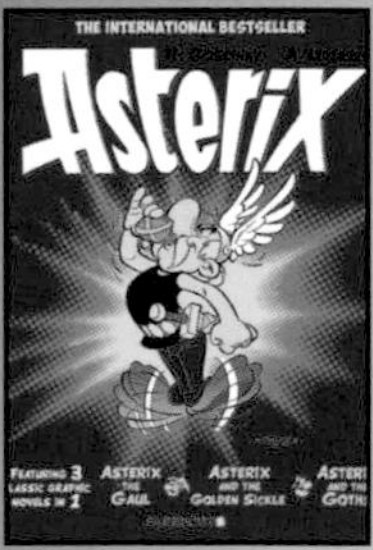
THE INTERNATIONAL BESTSELLER
Asterix
ASTERIX

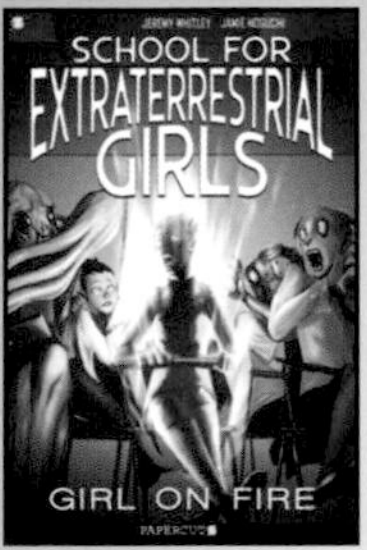
SCHOOL FOR EXTRATERRESTRIAL GIRLS
GIRL ON FIRE
PAPERCUTZ
SCHOOL FOR EXTRATERRESTRIAL GIRLS

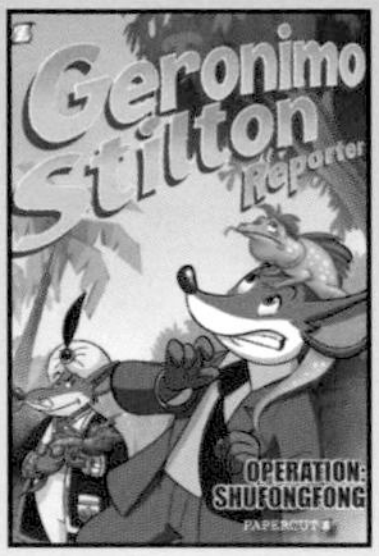
Geronimo Stilton
Reporter
OPERATION: SHUFONGFONG
PAPERCUTZ
GERONIMO STILTON REPORTER

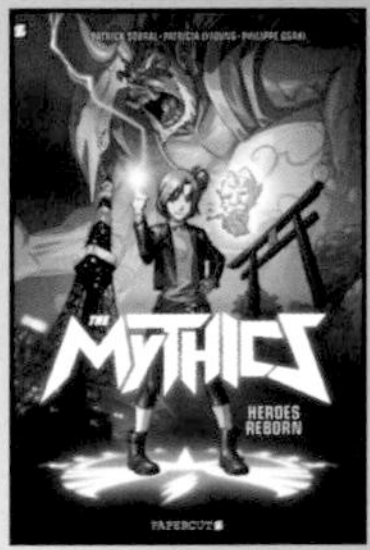
THE MYTHICS
HEROES REBORN
PAPERCUTZ
THE MYTHICS

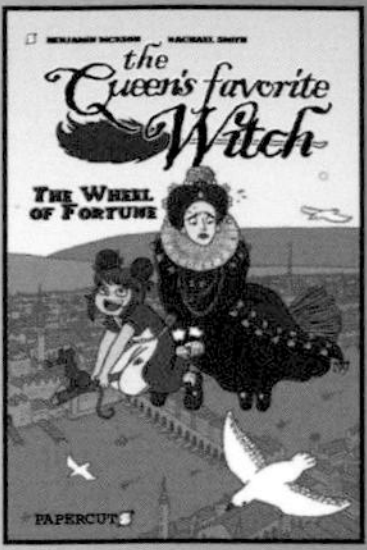
the Queen's favorite Witch
THE WHEEL OF FORTUNE
PAPERCUTZ
THE QUEEN'S FAVORITE WITCH

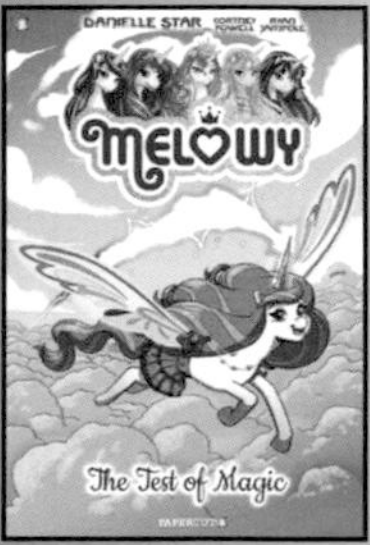
DANIELLE STAR
Melowy
The Test of Magic
PAPERCUTZ
MELOWY

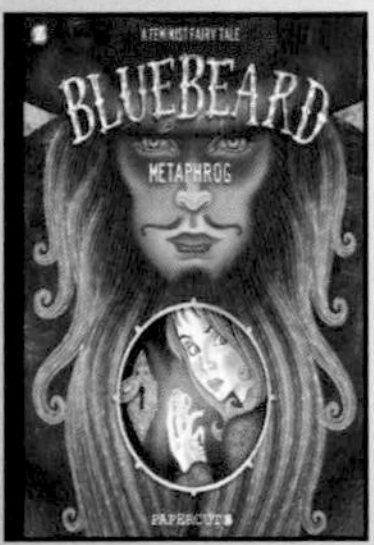
A FEMINIST FAIRY TALE
BLUEBEARD
METAPHROG
PAPERCUTZ
BLUEBEARD

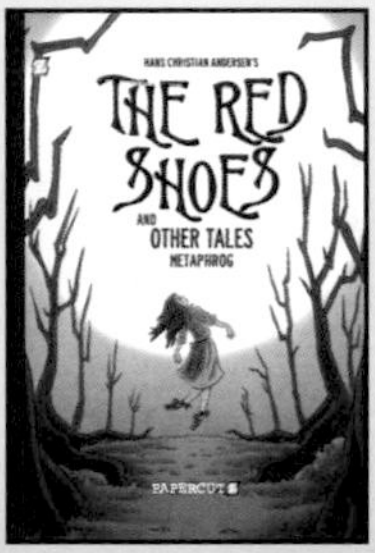
HANS CHRISTIAN ANDERSEN'S
THE RED SHOES
AND OTHER TALES
METAPHROG
PAPERCUTZ
THE RED SHOES

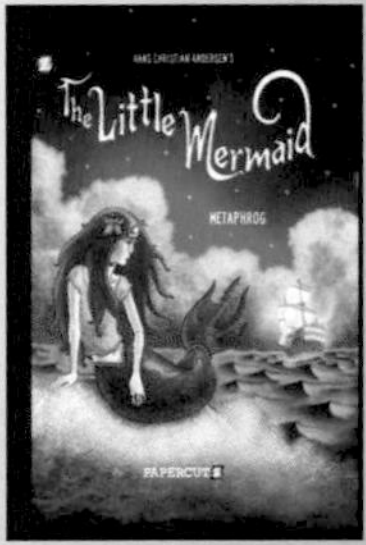
HANS CHRISTIAN ANDERSEN'S
The Little Mermaid
METAPHROG
PAPERCUTZ
THE LITTLE MERMAID

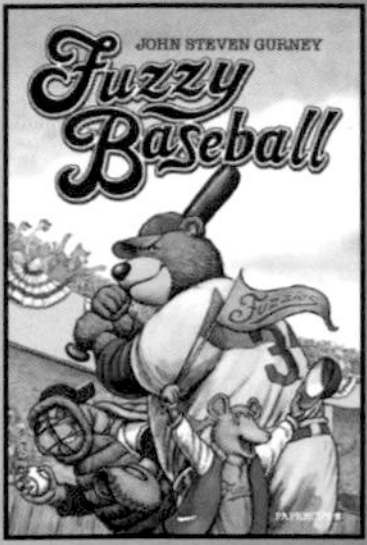
JOHN STEVEN GURNEY
Fuzzy Baseball
FUZZY BASEBALL

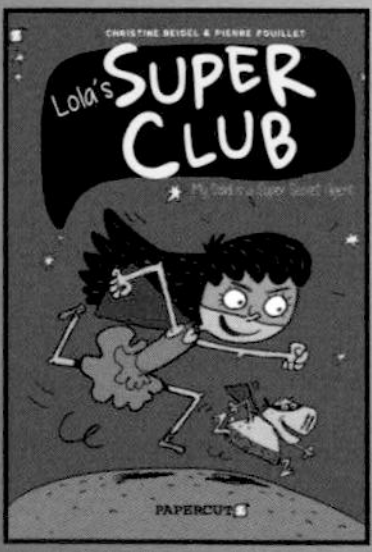
CHRISTINE BEIGEL & PIERRE FOUILLET
Lola's SUPER CLUB
PAPERCUTZ
LOLA'S SUPER CLUB

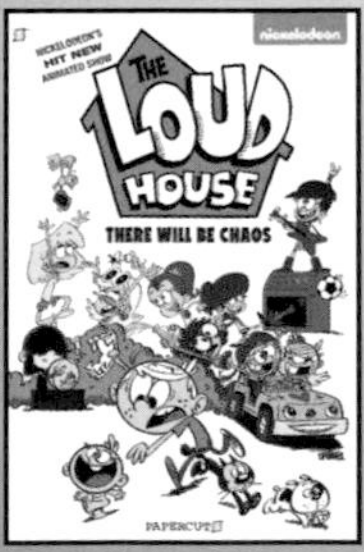
nickelodeon
THE LOUD HOUSE
THERE WILL BE CHAOS
PAPERCUTZ
THE LOUD HOUSE

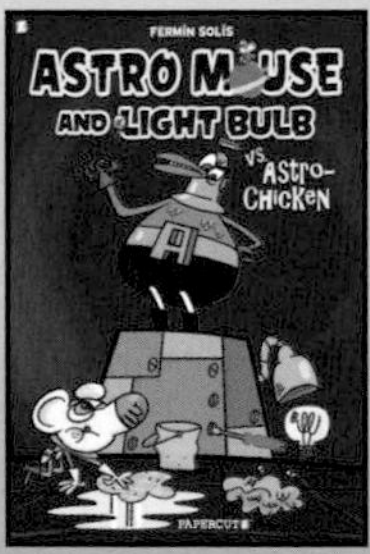
FERMÍN SOLÍS
ASTRO MOUSE AND LIGHT BULB
VS ASTRO-CHICKEN
PAPERCUTZ
ASTRO MOUSE AND LIGHT BULB

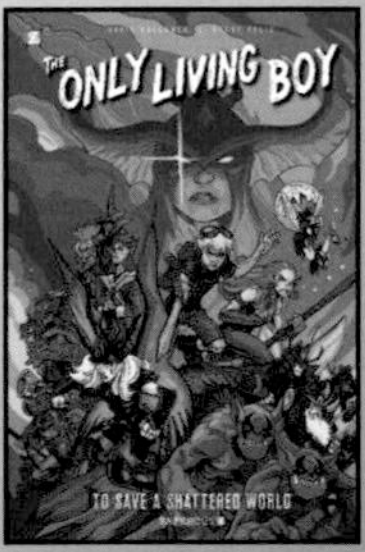
THE ONLY LIVING BOY
TO SAVE A SHATTERED WORLD
THE ONLY LIVING BOY

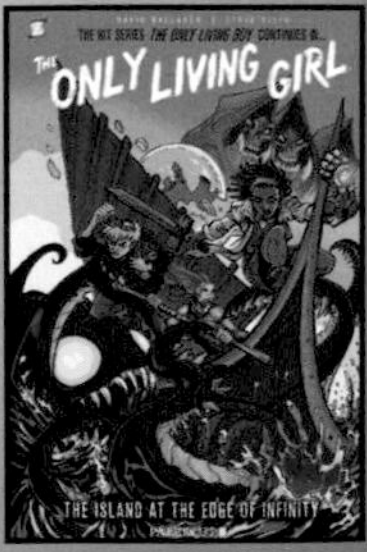
THE ONLY LIVING GIRL
THE ISLAND AT THE EDGE OF INFINITY
THE ONLY LIVING GIRL

papercutz.com

Also available where ebooks are sold.